PAPER SHERIFF

Also by Luke Short
in Thorndike Large Print

Ride the Man Down
Ambush
And the Wind Blows Free
Bounty Guns
The Branded Man
Donovan's Gun
First Campaign
The Guns of Hanging Lake
Last Hunt
The Man on the Blue
Marauders' Moon
Play a Lone Hand
Ram Rod
Sunset Graze
Hardcase

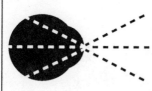 This Large Print Book carries the
Seal of Approval of N.A.V.H.

PAPER SHERIFF

LUKE SHORT

Thorndike Press • Thorndike, Maine

Library of Congress Cataloging in Publication Data:

Short, Luke, 1908–1975.
  Paper sheriff / Luke Short.
      p. cm.
  ISBN 1-56054-232-2 (alk. paper : lg. print)
  1. Large type books. I. Title.
[PS3513.L68158P36   1992]   91-34106
813'.54—dc20   CIP

Thorndike Press Large Print edition published in 1992
by arrangement with Kate Hirson and Daniel Glidden.

Cover design by James B. Murray.

The tree indicium is a trademark of Thorndike Press.

This book is printed on acid-free, high opacity paper.

PAPER SHERIFF

1

In the stifling June day court-room the Judge, distaste in his gaunt, exhausted face, addressed the all male jury.

"Normally, at the end of a long trial I thank the members of the jury for their patience and for their honest effort to arrive at a just decision. Eight of you men I do thank. Four of you will never receive my thanks."

He leaned back in his chair and seemed to welcome its support. "You four have totally disregarded the sworn evidence of your elected Sheriff as well as the evidence of other witnesses. I can only believe this was done wilfully. By doing so you have made a mockery of justice."

Now he put both his hands flat on the bench and leaned forward. "I think I know why you did it. The Assistant District Attorney is a woman prosecuting this case because her father, the District Attorney, was too ill to appear in court. To you she did not represent the court. She was only a lowly woman trying to get a man hanged. The court-room is no scene for the battle of the sexes, but you four took it upon yourselves to make it one. As a consequence, the jury could not agree and the defendant goes free. I doubt if you even feel ashamed — but I assure you I do." He paused. "Bailiff, free the prisoner. The jury is dismissed; the court is adjourned." He gavelled once sharply but the sound of it was lost in the uproar of the court-room.

The hard-packed earth in front of the stone Sutton County Court House was soon thronged by the crowd who had witnessed the trial. They seemed reluctant to leave. The last act of the drama was yet to come — the sight of a man they thought as good as dead walking down the Court House steps a free man. Men in worn range clothes, men in bib overalls, men in proper suits and their womenfolk, all waited for Orville Hoad, the man who shot Will Flowers in the back, to walk into the free summer sunshine.

When he did come out he was accompanied by his brother, Ty Hoad. Both men were middle-aged, but that was all, save their dark inheritance, they had in common. Orville Hoad, the taller and younger, had not bothered to clean up for his trial, as if it were of no consequence. He wore a dirty, collarless shirt, worn levis, scuffed cowman's boots and dusty Stetson, the clothes he had been arrested in two weeks before. His beard-stubbled face was long and the smile under his blade of a nose revealed stained and crooked teeth as he surveyed the scattered crowd.

Both men were met past the bottom of the steps by a half dozen men who moved forward in a group, shouting their pleasure. Ty Hoad stepped aside, smiling, so the men could take turns at wringing Orville's hand and clapping him on the back. Ty Hoad, dressed in the seedy propriety of a dark suit, was all chunky softness. The luxuriant pale moustaches only accentuated his buck teeth and gave him the appearance of a benevolent woodchuck. A yellowed panama hat and black string tie completed the illusion that this man might have been a visiting river boat pilot who had strayed a thousand miles from the broad Mississippi.

"Uncle Orv, you've got a fool's luck," one of the young men shouted drunkenly. He pushed a bottle toward Orville, who accepted it and took three long gulps of the pale raw moonshine. When he had got his breath, he said, "I been missin' that, Buddy."

To an observer watching this, the men around the Hoads would have seemed of a type. They were mostly lean, shabbily dressed, dirtier than necessary and in their unshaven faces was a pride of ignorance worn like a badge. They were all Hoads or married to Hoads and come to welcome one of themselves back into their shabby, whisky-sodden clan.

Buddy, facing Orville, now looked over his uncle's shoulder and said softly, "Oh, oh. Here comes Callie with her purty Sheriff." He pronounced it as if it were spelled "Shurf" Now he glanced at Ty Hoad. "Pa, you going to invite the Shurf to our party?"

Ty Hoad glanced sideways at the Court House steps where Sheriff Reese Branham and his wife Callie, Ty's daughter, were standing. Branham was a tall man with a dark and saturnine face which, at the sight of the Hoads, altered from its expression of sober friendliness into one of watchful reserve. He was dressed in a dark suit and tie, polished cowman's boots and an ancient, dust-colored Stetson. At thirty, he appeared to have the maturity and authority of an older man.

Even standing away from him, Callie Branham looked almost diminutive. She was a full-bodied girl, wearing a long-sleeved dress of blue print cotton that contrasted pleasantly with her thick reddish hair under its tiny bonnet. Hers was a Hoad face too, but a refined one — thin, without much color and with the sharply ridged nose separating pale eyes.

Now Callie tripped down the steps, ran up

10

to her uncle and embraced him affectionately. "Uncle Orv, I knew they wouldn't hang you, I just knew it!"

Orville Hoad looked past her to the Sheriff and said quietly, "They sure tried, Callie."

Now Reese Branham, his badge of office hidden by his coat, came slowly down the steps and approached the group, his grey eyes scanning each face, reading rightly in them the old dislike that now bordered on hatred.

Halting by his wife, Reese said, "Shall we go, Callie?" He didn't even look at Orville Hoad, who was watching him with a faint gleam of malice in his eyes.

"Aren't you going to say anything to Uncle Orv after what he's been through?" Callie asked.

"We've said enough to each other in the last two weeks. No."

"Ain't you going to shake his hand?" one of the Hoads jeered.

"Sure," Buddy said. "Reese only tried to hang him but he don't hold no hard feelings, do you, Uncle Orv? You'd be proud to shake the hand that would've put a rope around your neck, wouldn't you?"

"No, I think I'll use my hand to wrap around that bottle, Buddy. Give over."

Buddy handed back the bottle of moonshine and they watched the older man drink. The onlookers, satisfied that they had seen the disappointing last act of the drama, now began to drift away. Orville Hoad handed back the bottle, wiped his mouth on his shirtsleeve and said, "All you folks come over to my place now. We'll have us a celebration."

"The Sheriff too?" one of the Hoads asked slyly.

"Why, him too," Orville said sardonically. "Ain't he one of us Hoads through Callie? Don't us Hoads stick together and help each other? Ain't he been helping me this last two weeks, feeding me, keeping me out of the rain, watching over me, taking real good care of me? Why, I can't thank him enough. Sure, he's invited."

"I think I'll let Callie represent me, Orv. I've work to do tonight," Branham said.

"Well, now, that's too bad," Orville said. "I bet I know what you'll be working on. A frame for somebody else, now that you couldn't frame me."

"Wrong guess," Reese said patiently.

"Then maybe on that pretty woman lawyer," Orville said.

Instinctively, unthinkingly, Reese backhanded him with his right hand with such force that Orville had to take a step back to keep his balance.

With a surprising lack of anger, Orville said

12

quietly, "That must have come pretty close to where you live, Sheriff."

"No. I just don't like her name in your mouth."

Ty Hoad put his arm around his daughter's shoulders and said quickly, "I never like to see a ruckus around a woman. Now all of you quit. Let's move out to Orville's place." He squeezed Callie's shoulder. "If Reese has got to work, you come with me, Callie. Afterwards you can drop me off and take the buggy home." He looked at Reese now. "That all right with you, Reese?"

"Whatever Callie wants," Reese said indifferently.

"I'll be home in time to get your supper, Reese," Callie said.

All the Hoads, even Buddy and Orville, appeared satisfied with this compromise but each in his own way indicated to Reese by a look at him or at the others that this was at best a temporary truce. Branham turned and headed back for the Court House steps, with a premonition that would not be stifled. During the long days of Orville Hoad's trial, the testimony that he had been required to give had damned Hoad in the eyes of half the population of this county seat of Bale. Because he was married to a Hoad, he knew the Hoad clan, to a man, had expected him to lie unblushingly to protect one of the family. During the trial they had sat with mounting fury and hatred as he presented evidence of Orville's guilt and at the end of each court day they avoided him, losing themselves in the exiting crowd. They planned a reckoning with him, he knew, and didn't care. At the moment his bitter disappointment at the jury's actions was deep and sore. Mounting the steps, he tramped down the now empty corridor, heading for his office, a tall, tired man with rancor in his heart.

As he passed the open doors of the now empty court-room, he saw Judge Heatherly and Jen Truro seated at the defense's table, facing each other across it. Immediately Reese turned and walked into the court-room and the sound of his boots on the wood floor caused both Jen and Judge Heatherly to look in his direction. Reese took off his hat, walked through the gate in the railing and came up to the chair beside Jen Truro. She was watching him from wide-spaced eyes so black they were colorless. Her dark hair, a little dishevelled, framed a face that was now thoughtful and tired, holding a resignation that marred its almost classic beauty. She was dressed in a simple suit of dark grey with a white blouse underneath. She wore no jewelry and Reese knew that she had worn this unbecoming outfit during the long trial only because she did not want her clothes or her face to influence the jury and because this somber outfit looked as close to the lawyer's traditional dark suit as possible.

"Your father will be proud of you, Jen," Reese said.

"I'll see that Sebastian hears it in detail," Judge Heatherly said and gave Jen a wan, tired smile.

"Proud of me losing for him?" Jen asked quietly. "He's proud of a winner, not of a loser."

Reese pulled out one of the attorney's chairs beside Jen and slacked into it, looking over at Judge Heatherly. "I liked that benediction you aimed at the jury, Judge. You might have been speaking for me and for Jen."

Judge Heatherly grimaced. "I caught on to those four fairly early in the week. They never said a word, of course, but you could read it in their faces." He hesitated, musing for a few moments that were not interrupted. "There's a type of man who's born hating all women. As soon as he can walk, he resents their discipline and he escapes it as soon as he can. He's the kind that beats up women because that act proves to him that he's superior and they're inferior. He's the unsworn enemy of their sex — I say unsworn because he isn't conscious of despising them. That feeling is just part of him, like the act of breathing. He'll neither love nor respect a woman until the day he dies."

Now he looked at Jen with fondness and with sympathy. "You can't keep this kind of man off a jury, Jen. He wouldn't admit to this prejudice even if you asked him, because he doesn't know he has it. When he gives all the right answers to the questions put to him by attorneys for both sides, he's accepted as a responsible juror and seated." The Judge squared his hands in a gesture of helplessness and added, "Then what happened today is inevitable. Those four men weren't casting a ballot on the guilt or innocence of Orville Hoad. They were simply voting against a woman, all women."

Now he put his palms on the table and pushed himself upright. "I'm tired and at the moment I'm disgusted with the human race. And I'm sorry for you both." He picked up his hat and briefcase from the chair beside him. "Now I'll say goodbye."

They bid him goodbye and watched him as he tramped slowly down the hall and turned into the corridor.

Jen and Reese regarded each other for a moment and then Reese said, "I can understand why he feels sorry for you, but why should he include me?"

"Maybe for the same reason I feel sorry for you, Reese," Jen said quietly.

"And why do you?"

Jen shrugged slightly. "You're married into the Hoad family, Reese. I don't think they'll be forgiving."

"No, they won't," Reese said, just as quietly. "But as long as I know that, I can handle them."

"Is Callie bitter about it?"

Reese smiled crookedly. "Up until today she thought I was only doing my routine job. I haven't talked with her since I was on the stand this morning."

"Poor girl," Jen said softly. "It can't be easy for her, can it?"

Reese said dryly, "I can tell you that later."

Jen turned and picked up her black briefcase from the chair beside her. She said, without looking at Reese, "No, don't tell me later. I don't want to know."

"You'll know," Reese said. "You'll see it in me or in her and it won't change anything, will it?"

Jen stood up. "Nothing will," she said quietly. "I have to go, Reese."

Reese came to his feet and said, "Tell your father I'll be around tonight. Between the Judge and me we ought to convince him you're a passable lawyer."

For the first time that day Jen smiled. She said goodbye and Reese watched her leave the court-room, her back proud and straight once more, thanks mainly, he thought, to Judge Heatherly's words.

Reese sat down again, grateful for the silence and solitude of the empty court-room. He wanted to assess the importance of this day's events, now that the trial was over. The testimony that had been given this morning had been explosive and had seemingly assured Orville Hoad's conviction for murder in the first degree. It came from a surprise witness whom Jen and Reese had hunted down, questioned and then hidden. Orville Hoad had been charged with the murder of Will Flowers on a May night two weeks ago. The two men, both presumably drunk, had quarrelled openly at a card game at the Best Bet saloon.

The quarrel, which took place in the early hours of the morning, was broken up by the other card players before the two men could come to blows or gun play. Will Flowers, a heavy drinking, dryland farmer with a passion for gambling, never carried a gun. After the quarrel, the game broke up and Flowers headed for Hunter's Feed Stable to get his horse. Orville Hoad followed him minutes later, heading for the same

18

destination and on the same errand.

Orville Hoad's story was that Flowers waited for him in the stable back out of the light from the lantern hanging in the archway. Hoad maintained that Flowers took up a position at the entrance of a stall over whose partition some puncher had thrown his saddle. Over the horn of the saddle he had looped his shell belt and gun, a customary practice of cowhands who wanted to do some drinking but who wanted to stay out of a shooting spree. Hoad claimed that Flowers gave him a tongue-lashing in the half-lit stable, then turned to the shell belt and reached for the gun in its holster. Out of self-defense, Hoad pulled out his own gun and shot the half-turned Flowers before he was shot himself. There were no known witnesses and Hoad's story was plausible.

But Reese's persistent questioning of the day hostler at the stable had turned up the fact that a strange cow puncher that same evening had asked to sleep in the hayloft, was given permission, turned over his matches to the hostler and then had gone out into the town hunting for a saloon.

On a quiet and painstaking search, with only the hostler's description of the stranger to guide him, Reese had hit every town and ranch within a fifty-mile radius of Bale. He was looking for a recently hired hand. He turned up a dozen of them, but only one had fitted the description given by the hostler. Under Reese's questioning, this man finally admitted that he watched the shooting. Flowers, according to him, was searching the stalls for his horse when Orville Hoad came in and restarted their quarrel. He tried to goad Flowers into a fight, but Flowers had cooled off and wanted no more of their quarrel. When he turned away, Hoad shot him in the back. It was true the puncher had left his saddle, shell belt, and gun on the stall partition. Hoad had simply walked over to the stall, drawn out the gun, pitched it on the stable floor by Flowers' body and walked out. The stranger, afraid of what he had seen happen in a strange town, simply got his horse and rode out.

This morning Reese had taken the stand and stated simply that he had uncovered a witness to the murder. The stranger was put on the stand, gave his testimony, which was unshakable under the cross-examination, and afterwards Jen gave her summation.

Now, what was Callie Branham going to think of her husband, who had kept the secret of the murder witness from her, Reese wondered. She would think he had not trusted her and she would be right. Beyond that she would think he and Jen had secretly conspired to hang one of the Hoads and again she would be right.

Unconsciously he sighed and then rose, tramping back into the corridor, turning and going down it to his small office in the rear corner. As he stepped into the room he saw his deputy, Jim Daley, seated at the single roll top desk. At the sound of his entrance Jim Daley turned and the two men regarded each other silently. Daley was a stocky, middle-aged man, dressed in clean range clothes. Surmounting his broad, fight-scarred face was a thick mat of short-cut grey hair that burred out from a round skull. Now Daley said in a low-voiced, mocking drawl, "Bailiff, free the prisoner."

Reese smiled crookedly at his deputy's recollection of Judge Heatherly's orders. Daley was bailiff of the court and he was not likely ever to forget those words. Reese slacked into a chair beside the desk and said tiredly, "I guess I married into a lucky family, Jim."

"Any chance that family got to those four jurors, Reese?" Then he added, "Excuse the question, but is there?"

"It's possible, but I don't think so," Reese said gloomily. "I think, and so does the Judge, that they didn't like the idea of a woman trying to get a man hanged. You can add this too. I think they might have been afraid that the

21

Hoad clan would gun them down if they voted to hang Orville."

Daley, watching him carefully, opened his mouth to speak, then thought better of it. But he could not keep the pity out of his eyes and Reese, seeing it, was unaccountably angry. Judge Heatherly felt sorry for him, Jen felt sorry for him and now Jim Daley felt sorry for him, too. The anger died then and Reese rose. "Jim, the Hoads are celebrating tonight. They'll be liquored up and they may take a notion to come to town and crow. If they come in stay away from them, unless they get into some trouble you have to handle."

Daley nodded and said quietly, "They're an easy bunch to hate all right."

"And not worth risking your life for," Reese said dryly. "See you tomorrow, Jim."

Reese went out the corridor's rear door and headed for the open shed where the horses of the county employees were stabled. He saddled his grey gelding, then rode down the alley which led onto Bale's main street.

Normally he liked the sight of the wide street of false front buildings at this hour of the early evening. Businessmen, their stores locked up for the day, would wave to him on their way home. Kids, running on last minute errands, would call to him. The Best Bet, a big box of a saloon with a hotel in its second storey, would be cheerfully noisy. The horses and riders coming into town for the evening or leaving town for the night would have stirred up the dust that seemed yellow in the rays of the slanted sun. This same sun seemed to bring out the color in the few drably painted buildings and in the weathered wood of the unpainted ones.

But as he rode down the street now the town seemed to hold no charm or friendliness. For the first time since he was sworn into office he wondered why he had let his friends prevail upon him to run for sheriff. They had promised him that after they elected him he would become a "paper sheriff," a figurehead. He could hire himself a good deputy, they said, and go about his business of running his Slash Seven cattle outfit. What they were after, they told him, was a stockman sheriff, one of their own, not a miner's sheriff and not a soft sheriff who would take money and open up the town and attract a rough element by its easy reputation. But now, he thought morosely, he had been rewarded for his labors by this bitter farce of the Hoad trial.

His mood stayed with him for the two mile ride over rolling prairie grassland which brought him to his own fence and gate. The Slash Seven, the original Joe Bale ranch bought by his father, had the sprawling look of having been built by a man who wanted plenty of room. The big two-storey log house had single storey wings on the east and west sides and lay among giant cottonwoods so thickly foliaged that the flowers Callie planted had to fight for enough sun. It was a big house meant for a big family, Reese thought — a family it would never have. Reese rode past it and the cookshack-bunkhouse to the pasture gate where he unsaddled and turned out his grey. There was smoke coming from the chimney stack of the kitchen wing, and that meant Callie was home. A kind of quiet dread touched him as he moved toward the open kitchen door and stepped inside.

Callie was at the big iron stove against the far wall and Reese noted she had changed out of her blue dress into a drab and unbecoming brown one over which she now wore an apron. At his entrance she turned to look at him but did not speak. Reese nodded and said mildly, "Smells good in here."

He shucked out of his coat and hung it and his hat on a nail beside the door, then moved over to the sink. As he took down the wash basin and filled it from the sink pump, he said, "You didn't have to come home to get my supper, Callie. Why didn't you stay?"

"I wanted to," Callie said shortly.

Reese glanced at her swiftly, searchingly,

and he could tell that the color in her usually wan cheeks did not come from the heat of the stove but from the Hoads' moonshine. He untied his tie, rolled up his sleeves and was soaping his face when Callie said from close behind him, "I wanted to stay, but I came home. Remember that, will you?"

Reese rinsed his face, reached for a towel and then, drying himself, turned to Callie. "All right, but why?"

There was anger in Callie's face, he saw, and he could smell the rank odor of whisky on her breath.

"You'll find out," she said enigmatically.

She went back to the stove and now Reese, after hanging up the towel, moved over to the cupboard, took down a bottle of whisky and a glass and poured himself a drink.

"Make me one too," Callie said.

Wordlessly, Reese took down a second glass, poured a drink, then moved with both glasses over to the pump and splashed water into them. He could not yet fathom Callie's mood nor the meaning of her words, but he knew she was laying the groundwork for something special. Moving across the room he extended Callie's drink to her and then lifted his own. It had barely touched his lips when he saw Callie move swiftly. A fraction of a second later he caught the full force of

Callie's drink in his face. Slowly he wiped his eyes with his sleeve and then very calmly threw the contents of his own drink in Callie's face.

Callie gasped with shock and Reese said quietly, "Smarts the eyes, doesn't it?" He turned now and went back to the counter, towelled himself, poured another drink, mixed water with it, then turned to watch Callie. She was wiping her face with a dish-towel and was at the same time crying.

"Pa would shoot you for that!" Callie said furiously.

"He'd probably shoot me for less than that," Reese said contemptuously. "Now let's talk this out, Callie, not fight it out. What's wrong?"

"You ask that?" Callie said hotly. "After trying to hang my uncle, after keeping secrets from me along with that bitch of a woman, you ask me that?"

"Callie, your uncle killed a man. You heard how he killed him this morning. And when you kill a man in the way he did, you hang for it."

"Why did you hunt up this cowboy that said he saw Uncle Orville shoot Will Flowers?" Callie demanded angrily. Then she said, "You and Jen Truro paid him to say that, didn't you?"

"Is that what your family thinks? Is that what you think?"

"We think Uncle Orville shot him in a fair fight, just like he said!"

"That cow puncher was telling the truth, Callie. Nobody paid him anything."

"Maybe you didn't, but can you prove that damn woman of yours didn't?"

Reese set down his drink. " 'That woman of yours,' " he echoed. "Callie, I've got one woman. You."

"That you wish you didn't have," Callie said hotly.

Reese said, "That's right."

"Well, you've got me and I've got you," Callie said. "I'll keep you too."

"I reckon you will," Reese said, as if to himself.

"Do you know how I'll keep you?" Callie asked vengefully. "By doing everything a wife should do. I came home to get your supper tonight, didn't I? Do you want to go to bed with me? Let's go in the bedroom. Do you want to make a baby? Let's make a baby. Is there anything you want from me?"

"No," Reese said gently. "Nothing, Callie."

"You see, I'll never give you cause to divorce me," Callie said angrily. "You can leave me for that damn woman if you want, but I don't think you will. She'll want you married

27

to her, and you're married to me and always will be."

Reese said quietly, "It's not much of a marriage for you, is it, Callie?"

Callie said, suddenly sober, "It's nothing. You could make it something, but you won't."

"We made a mistake, Callie."

"You made the mistake," Callie said flatly. "You wanted me and I let you have me because I loved you. I could still love you, only you won't let me."

Reese reached for his drink, lifted it and looked over the glass at his wife. Everything she said was true, he thought, but her saying it didn't change anything. He felt a sudden pity for her that was flawed by contempt. She was acting as she had been taught to act by her family clan — with loyalty, headlong temper and vindictiveness. She could not help herself nor could he help her. He took a sip of his drink and put his glass down very gently, watching it as if he thought it might break. Then he looked up at her. "I'm only being honest, Callie."

"Then be dishonest!" Callie cried. "Pretend you love me! Pretend we have a good marriage! Pretend you like my family! Pretend you want a dozen kids! Pretend you're alive, because you're only going through the motions of living now!" Then she added in a small, dismal voice, "Like me."

Reese said tonelessly, "That wouldn't work, Callie, and you're smart enough to know it."

"It wouldn't work?" Callie asked fiercely. "It's the only thing that *will* work! You're my man, you're married to me and you'll stay married to me. Make the best of it, Reese. If you'll try, I'll try."

Reese straightened up and said quietly, "It's no use, Callie. Let's have supper."

"Your supper's in the oven. I don't want any." Callie moved swiftly into the living room and Reese heard the sound of her heel taps crossing it, followed by the sound of the door to the bedroom shutting.

Now he drained off his drink and poured himself another, wondering what had brought this to a head tonight. He suspected that it was because he and Jen had kept the secret of a witness whose testimony should have hanged Orville Hoad. Had he ever told Callie that he loved Jen Truro? He didn't have to, he supposed wryly. At one time the whole town, the whole county knew it, so why shouldn't Callie have known it?

Jen had known twice and she knew it now, just as she knew the unlovely history of his marriage to Callie Hoad. That marriage had happened two years ago when, like a fool, he had chosen the path of honor that had led to this misery. He could not remember when he had first loved Jen. Perhaps it was when she came back from college to read law in her father's office, determined to become a lawyer. At least that was when he proposed to her the first time. Jen had put him off, saying that while she loved him, she first wanted to study under her father and be admitted to the Bar. He had agreed to wait, watching with both amazement and amusement while she fought and clawed for her right to take the Bar examination, which she passed so brilliantly that she could not be denied admittance to the Bar and the right to practice as the first woman lawyer in the State's history.

Looking back at it, he supposed the turning point was the paralytic stroke suffered by Sebastian Truro, Jen's father. Her mother was long dead and there was no one to take care of him and his law practice except Jen. When he proposed for the second time, even the tenth time, he received the same answer — her father needed her and she had no right to carry the burden of an invalid father into their marriage.

It was after this tenth refusal that Reese, in rage and frustration, had made up his mind to forget her. He had met Callie Hoad at a Fourth of July dance and thought her refreshingly unlike the other Hoads. She and her father were newly come to the country to join the clan of the less prosperous Hoads. He began half-heartedly courting Callie, more to spite Jen than because of his love for Callie. It was just as Callie said, she loved him and, inevitably, too well. When she became pregnant by him, he had offered marriage and she had accepted. Four months later she miscarried their child.

This, Reese supposed, was the history of half the marriages in the Christian world; it could almost be called the human condition. Women married men they didn't really love in order to protect their good names, and men married women they were only momentarily fond of in order to save them from disgrace. They accepted what fate or nature handed them — a partner for life, children to raise and a companionship of sorts, tempered by quarrels, reconciliations and monotony.

This acceptance, of course, was what Callie expected of him and against which his whole being revolted. Part of his reason for agreeing to run for Sheriff had been to get away from her and from the smothering idiocy of the Hoad clan. Callie, he found, didn't consider herself an individual, only a member of the family that could do no wrong. Originally the Hoads had come from the hill country of Tennessee — a hard-drinking, hard-bargaining, hard-fighting and hard-luck clan who attributed their own survival to the fact they were one united and loyal family. They were as alien to him as a group of Australian bushmen and hardly more understandable.

He finished his drink, then picked up the bottle to pour himself another. He hesitated, bottle in hand, and then with a kind of self-loathing, he put down the bottle and corked it. He couldn't change any of this by crawling into a bottle, he thought wryly. *I'm like a lone man, heading into the desert, leading a horse that's carrying plenty of food and water. I have to go, but I don't know where I'm going.*

At that moment he knew the deepest loneliness.

Ty and Orville Hoad sat in rocking chairs on the veranda of Orville's peeled log house, a jug of pale whisky between them, watching the dusk slowly fade into the night. Buddy, after taking his sister Callie home, had returned and he, his cousins, Junior and Emmett and Big John, all Orville's boys, partly sobered up by the supper just finished, had taken off for town to continue their celebration. Min, Orville's wife, had cleaned up and gone immediately to bed so that the two brothers were alone for the first time that day. Orville's chair was on a squeaky board and he hitched it forward, then stretched out his long legs which he crossed at the ankles.

"Ty, I done me some thinking these last couple of weeks. Lordy, I had enough time to do it."

"About hanging?"

"Some, I reckon, but mostly what I was going to do if I got off."

"You can't be that lucky twice, Orv," Ty said dryly.

"You're wrong, Ty, I can," Orville said flatly. He looked at his brother. "You ain't thought much about what happened today, have you?"

"Only that at one time this morning I thought you were as good as dead. What should I've been thinking about?"

"Why, the reason I got off."

"That's easy. Like I said, anybody with eyes could see it. Four of them jurymen from over south didn't like being told what to do by a woman."

"Me, I've been thinking past that," Orville said proudly. "Way, way past that."

"Like what?"

"Well, if that lady lawyer couldn't hang me, then who'll she ever get a conviction against so long as there's a jury there?"

Ty grunted in surprise. What Orville said was true and he hadn't thought of it that way. He leaned down now, lifted the jug from beside his yellowed panama on the porch floor and took a drink of the fiery whisky, put back the corn cob cork and offered the jug to Orville, who only shook his head. Ty put the jug back beside his hat, feeling the rich warmth of the whisky churn around his supper. He said, "Supposing that's true?"

Orville laughed silently. "Me, I'm not going to keep scratching so hard. I aim to have me a little cash money coming in. I aim to buy more range that will run more cows." He looked at Ty. "You got more'n me, Ty, but you got enough? You got all you want? You want to get more?"

"Any man does. What d'you have in mind?"

Orville leaned forward now. He pointed loosely out into the lowering night. "Forty miles yonder is the National Trail. Those big Texas herds will be coming up all summer. There's enough of us Hoads to make up a bunch, Ty. We could stampede every other herd and we got the men to round up and drive off part of every herd. We move in quick up into the mountains."

"I know what's coming," Ty said dryly. "You want my line cabin and corrals in Copper Canyon."

"Why, surely," Orville said. "There's room to handle them and grass to hold them. As soon as the brands are healed over we drive them down the other side of the mountain and sell them in Grant County and Jefferson and Moffitt."

Ty thought a minute and then said, "Yes, but it's risky, Orv. Those Texans are mean and tough."

"I'm meaner and tougher than any Texan I ever seen," Orv said placidly. He paused. "It ain't as risky as you think, Ty, because we're safe here."

"Reese, you mean?"

"Hell, no, I don't mean Reese. He ain't one of us Hoads."

"Then how are we safe?"

"Callie," Orville said simply.

It was too dark for Ty to see Orville's face but he looked toward him anyway. "What's she got to do with it?"

"We organize a cattle company with Callie as head. She signs all the bills of sale. She's the buyer and the seller."

"But why Callie? Why not you or me?"

"You don't see it," Orville said sadly. "Why, it's as simple as this: Callie's Reese's wife. He'll think a long time before arresting her, but even if he does she's safe enough."

"How d'you figure that?"

35

"A woman can't testify against her husband and a husband can't testify against his wife. If he gets one of us, there's that lady lawyer again. Besides, we'd be stealing from Texans and that ain't really stealing to a Sutton County jury. See what we got working for us?"

Ty reviewed Orville's reasoning. "He can't get at Callie, no jury will convict a man Jen Truro is prosecuting and we don't like Texans."

It was Orville's turn to take a drink now and he did. When he could talk again, he said, "Yep. Find any holes in it?"

"Reese could deputize other men to gather evidence against us."

"They'll be plumb hard to hire," Orville said gently. "There's plenty of us Hoads and we ain't soft. Let Reese try to find the Hoad that shoots a deputy or a witness."

Ty thought carefully now. The time Buster Hoad had been dragged by a horse and killed, they had counted twenty-three Hoads by blood or marriage who attended Buster's funeral. Yes, as Orville said, there were plenty of Hoads to take care of any trouble that came up. All in all, it was a good scheme. It would take nerve and endurance, two qualities the Hoads had a plenty. The only question was, would Callie throw in with them and agree to act as responsible owner? She and Reese, Ty knew, were not getting along. They had fallen out of love or whatever it was that kept a man and his woman together, but how far out of love had Callie fallen? he wondered. Then he said aloud, "All right, Orv. I'll talk with Callie. You talked this over with the boys?"

"No. I was waiting on what you thought of it."

"Wait a little longer till I see where Callie stands. Without her it's no good."

"No," Orville agreed.

It was fully dark but not late when Reese stepped out of the stable and tied his horse to the ring held by a cast iron Negro in livery that stood before the white-painted small house of Sebastian Truro. The house looked as if it had been moved from a New England town, trim, a little stark and handsome. Reese opened the gate in the wrought iron fence, and as he tramped up the brick walk he could see through the wide bay window that Sebastian Truro was still up and in his wheelchair. Jen was standing talking to him and Reese noted with relief that she had changed out of her drab court-room costume into a dress that was near red in color. It was, he supposed, her protest against what she had worn the whole week.

Jen answered his knock and stepped aside as Reese returned her smile.

"It's been a while since I've seen you, Jen," Reese said dryly.

"Well, where've you been keeping yourself, Reese?" Jen answered and they both laughed. They stepped through the wide door of the parlor together and Reese crossed the room to where Sebastian Truro's wheelchair rested in the bay of the window.

Truro had been a theatrically handsome man before his stroke — white-haired with matching, unstained moustaches under a strong, arching nose. Now his lean face held an odd upward twist of the mouth so that he always seemed to be faintly smiling. His useless left hand lay shrivelled on the arm of his wheelchair. He was dressed as if he had just come home from his law office in a dark suit and flowing black tie; well polished boots hid the fact that his left foot and leg were also shrunken. Oddly his skin, instead of holding an invalid's pallor, was so suntanned that it bespoke many outdoor hours seated in the health-giving sunlight. At Reese's approach his dark eyes lighted up with pleasure and he extended his right hand.

"Counsellor, I hope you and Jen celebrated tonight."

"We did," Truro said. He hesitated and

then said abruptly, "We had a bottle of good wine."

Reese was used to this hesitance which seemed to be the only impediment in Truro's speech. It was as if he had to wait to gather some inner strength to form the words. This, Reese knew, was what kept Truro out of the court-room rather than the fact that he would have to appear in a wheelchair.

Jen had come up beside him now and Reese glanced down at her. "Let me tell you some things she's probably too modest to mention."

"Sit down, Reese, and stop talking about me. I wish I could wipe the whole trial from my mind."

Reese sat down in an upholstered rocking chair close to Truro and began to tell him of this day in court. First on the stand was Orville Hoad; arrogant, supremely confident, he had answered Jen with a maddening condescension, time and again calling her Missie as if she was a little girl and then apologizing to the court for his slip of the tongue. He seemed cross about the fact that he had even been held for trial. It was a pure case of kill or be killed. Was he supposed to hunt up a witness before he shot in self-defense? he asked. If he had taken time to do that, there would be no trial at all because he would be dead. Jen, Reese said, had made no objection to his rambling, self-righteous account of what took place in the livery stable. Her only questions were to ask for more exact details of where each man stood and what each man said. When Hoad was excused he seemed surprised, perhaps at the gentle treatment he had received at Jen's hands.

After Orville, Reese said, he himself had been called to the stand. Under Jen's questioning he told of the search for the cowboy who had slept in the stable, a drifter, whose name when found turned out to be Shep Humphrey.

It was Humphrey's testimony, brought out skilfully by Jen, that shattered the court-room silence. The defense in the cross-examination could not attack Humphrey's character because until that moment they had not known he existed. Hoad's lawyer had tried to make a liar out of him and failed miserably. They tried to smear his character and failed in that too. Finally, in desperation, Hoad's lawyers asked that the trial be recessed so that they could investigate the character of the witness. Judge Heatherly refused, the witness was excused and the court recessed for the noon hour. When court convened in the afternoon, Jen gave the summation, Reese said. It was given without histrionics, but the cold, unassailable facts were reviewed. Because there were no extenuating circumstances the jury was asked to return a verdict of murder in the first degree.

Counsel for the defense in his summation could only hint that in the past some member of the numerous Hoad family had injured Shep Humphrey and this fantastic and untrue story was his method of getting even.

It took the jury only an hour to agree that they could not and never would be able to agree on Orville Hoad's guilt or innocence.

When Reese finished Sebastian looked at Jen with both pride and affection. He started to speak, hesitated again, then said, "Very clever, Jen, your handling of Orville on the stand. It sounds as if he expected to be cut down to size and was surprised that he wasn't. In any other court of law you'd have got your conviction."

"Only if she had worn pants and grown a moustache," Reese said dryly. "I don't think we'd like her that way, would we, Counsellor?"

They all laughed and now Jen rose from her chair and said, "I'll make some coffee for us," before she turned and left the room. When she had gone, Truro opened his mouth to speak, paused, and then the words came. "I know the Hoads, Reese. They won't be easy on you from now on. In fact they'll be harder on you than if you weren't married to one of them."

Reese shrugged, his dark face suddenly somber, and then he said with a wry attempt at humor, "You can say one thing for me, Counsellor. When I buy into something, I buy in all the way."

"I wish you never had," Truro said abruptly. "I blame myself mostly for the fact you did. If it hadn't been for this cursed stroke and Jen's equally cursed sense of duty, you wouldn't be tangled with the Hoads."

"It's done," Reese said quietly. "Done and damned."

Jen came in with the coffee, interrupting their conversation about Judge Heatherly's chances of being nominated for a Senate seat. She joined in the discussion as they drank their coffee. Afterwards Jen declared it was bedtime for her father, the men shook hands and Jen wheeled her father down the corridor to his bedroom in back.

While she was gone, Reese slowly paced the living room, unconsciously making a game of stepping on the same patterns of the rug on each round. The problem of Callie was still sore in his mind. Following her outburst this evening, what could they expect in the future? Would it settle back into that grey tolerance the Hoad trial had shattered or would Callie nourish that vindictiveness she had revealed in their quarrel?

Jen returned and Reese stopped his pacing and watched her sit down. He hadn't known that she had been watching him from the corridor door for a full minute until she said, "You've been pacing this room like a tiger in a cage, Reese. Something troubling you?"

"Only the usual. Callie and I had a quarrel. She threw a glass of whisky in my face and I threw one in hers." He grimaced. "It was pretty sorry."

"Was I involved, Reese?" Jen asked curiously.

Reese nodded. "Whenever we quarrel, you're always involved. Callie can never understand that I have to work with the District Attorney's office and that that means you."

"Does she think we're lovers?"

Reese hesitated. "I reckon," he said slowly. "She puts herself in your place, Jen. She thinks that if she were you, we'd be lovers." He added wryly, "Remember, I was her lover before I was her husband."

Jen looked at him thoughtfully. "Well, we know we aren't lovers, Reese, much as we'd like to be. Then she can't hurt us."

"Maybe she can't but watch out, Jen. I can't stop her imagining things. If she imagines you're trying to get me away from her, there'll be trouble, real trouble."

"If I pretended to dislike you, would it help?"

"It's too late for that," Reese said quietly. His faint smile held no humor in it as he said, "It's too late for everything, I guess."

"Don't say that," Jen said quietly. "Don't —"

A distant gunshot out in the town overrode what she was about to say. It was followed by two more shots, then three more.

Reese scooped up his hat from the chair as Jen rose. "That's more than two men shooting at each other, Reese."

"Yes," Reese said. He moved swiftly to the door, opened it, took the steps in one leap, yanked his grey's reins from the tie-ring and vaulted into the saddle. More shots came now and from the direction of the Best Bet Saloon.

Reese touched spurs to his grey, who immediately stretched into a gallop. The Best Bet was two blocks from Truro's house and, like it, in the middle of a block. When Reese reached the main street, he checked his horse down to a trot, then swung around the corner. Two shots came from the building beyond the Best Bet, apparently the blacksmith shop, and were answered by a gun flare from across the street. Someone, Reese saw, was forced up in the narrow area between O'Connors' Saddle Shop and the Hale Mercantile across the street in mid-block. Now more shots came from beyond the Best Bet and further down the street a couple of horses at the tie-rail in front of the saloon were rearing against their reins. The other horses on both sides were shying away from them and into neighboring mounts. Again the gun by the saddle shop answered. Some one bellowed, "Shove out Buddy, Jim, and we'll let you go."

"If you hurt him, we'll kill you," another voice shouted angrily.

The Hoads, Reese knew. If he could piece this together from the two calls shouted across the street, then Jim Daley had Callie's brother Buddy in custody and the Hoads were trying to free one of their own.

At sight of Reese the firing ceased and now he rode up to the saddle shop and called out, "You all right, Jim?"

"Yes, watch out. I'm coming out," Daley answered.

"You stay there."

"There are three of them, Reese. Orville's boys. I'll put Buddy in front of me."

Reese repeated in a tone of iron, "You stay there." Now he swivelled his head trying to pick out the Hoads. In the faint light cast by the lamps from the Best Bet he could make out the partly closed doors of the blacksmith's shop and the iron watering trough abutting the break in the tie-rail for the driveway into the building. Stepping out of his saddle now, he let the reins of his grey drop, thus positioning his horse so as to block effective firing at Jim Daley. As he moved toward the shop a murmuring of voices from inside the blacksmith shop came to him. He had no intention of exposing Jim Daley to those three, for this, he knew, was directed at him personally. As he strode slowly forward, he called, "Come out of there! Or I'll come in after you!"

Again he heard a muttered conversation behind the doors and he kept tramping slowly forward until he was almost abreast of the watering trough. The hulking figure rose from behind it where he had taken shelter. From the size of him, Reese knew this was Big John, Orville's oldest boy.

"That's far enough, Cousin," Big John said, his voice thick with liquor. "Just backtrack to that horse and get out of here."

"Or you'll do what?" Reese asked quietly.

Big John lurched a step closer. "Just blow your head off, that's all."

Reese said coldly, "You're too drunk to blow out a candle, Big John, but try me on for size. I've got a dead Hoad owed me after today. It might as well be you." Now he moved slowly, changing direction, walking toward Big John.

"Get him, June!" Big John called to his brother.

Obediently Junior Hoad called from inside the shop in a wild and high voice, "Back off, Reese. Back off, I say."

Stubbornly Reese kept moving toward Big John. A scare shot flared from inside the blacksmith's shop and Reese heard the thud of a slug on the iron tank. While Big John was still startled, Reese lunged. His left hand came down on Big John's forearm and then he half-turned his own body, his arm pulling Big John's gun hand past him. Reese's shoulder caught Big John's chest in a savage drive that tipped the huge man off balance. He staggered a step backward and the rim of the watering trough caught him behind the knee. He fell into the trough, jack-knifed, his gun arm tearing loose from Reese's grip, and then over the sound of the splash Reese heard the dull thud of Big John's head hitting the far edge of the trough. That same moment his gun, pointed in the air and triggered by the reflex of the blow, went off harmlessly.

Reese wheeled now and took the three steps that brought him against the door of the blacksmith's shop. Drawing his gun, he flattened against the door, reached out his left hand and walked the sliding door back until the whole entrance was a gaping black hole. He looked now at Big John, who was sitting in the trough, knees hanging over, chin on chest, his mouth almost in the water. He was unconscious, Reese guessed, and that gave him an idea.

"Take a look at your big brother, June," Reese called.

"Get him out of there," Junior called in the same wild, high-pitched voice.

"He's drowning," Reese called. "Come out and get him, both of you. Throw out your guns first."

"You'll cut down on us!" a new voice said angrily. This was Emmett, the middle brother.

"On my own family?" Reese called mockingly. "Throw out your guns and get Big John out."

There was only the slightest hesitation and then one gun arced out, followed immediately by the second. Reese waited then as the two Hoads ran past him toward the trough, and while they each took one of Big John's arms and hauled him out of the trough, Reese picked up their two guns from the street. Turning then he saw that Junior and Emmett had set Big John's slack body upright on the edge of the tank and were holding him there. As Reese moved toward them, he heard Junior say solemnly, "Hell, his head wasn't even under water."

Reese couldn't see the expressions on their faces in the half-light, but he didn't have to.

Junior, in his twenties, was lean and mean-looking and had the same blade of a nose as his father. Emmett, a year older than Junior's twenty, was a short chunk of a young man who was never without a wad of tobacco bulging in his downy cheek. Between the two of them they had never spent a day in school.

Reese turned now and called, "Jim, bring Buddy over."

Seconds later Jim appeared, prodding Buddy ahead of him with his gun. The sight of them coming out of hiding was the signal for the patrons of the Best Bet to hit the boardwalk; a dozen of them tramped down to where Reese and the two Hoads were holding up Big John.

Jim Daley hauled up beside Reese and shoved Buddy, staggering drunk, toward his cousins.

"What started this?" Reese asked.

"They figured to wreck the Best Bet. Buddy was the worst, so I buffaloed him and hauled him out. Them three was going to take him away from me."

Reese looked at Buddy who was holding his neckerchief to his still bleeding head. He had Callie's reddish hair and sallow skin, but he was a big-boned, feisty man who, Reese judged, probably jeered in his sleep.

"Well, you got yourself some company,

Buddy. The three of you load him up. One take his feet, one grab his belt, one take his shoulders."

"And take him where?" Buddy asked sullenly.

"Where you were going to start with, jail," Reese said. He turned to Daley. "Get them moving, Jim. I'll be along with your horse. Where is it?"

Daley told him and now Reese shouldered through the silent bystanders. As Reese passed through he heard one man say, "That jail's turning into a boarding house for them damn Hoads."

His companion said, "More like a home, seems to me."

Tramping across the street, Reese mounted his horse and turned it around to pick up Daley's mount at the Best Bet tie-rail. Ty, Orville and Callie, of course, would blame him for this evening. He could almost hear them telling each other that it was a sorry day when four young fellows couldn't do a little sociable celebrating. He picked up Daley's horse and then, leading him, headed back toward the court-house. In this single day, he reflected, he had managed to alienate all the Hoads, and that included his wife.

Ty Hoad arrived at the Slash Seven in the

mid-morning, reasonably sure that Reese would not be home and that Callie would. Earlier Buddy had come back to Ty's Diamond T after his night in jail and told Ty of his and his cousins' arrest. Buddy was mad and hung over and outraged as were his three cousins, even though Jim Daley and Reese had filed no charges against them, letting them sleep off their drunk before freeing them.

By Ty's calculation, this would be a most appropriate time to deal with Callie, and when he rode up to the big house in the warm and windy morning, the place seemed deserted. Reese, he reckoned, had work to catch up on after the trial and was probably out with his crew. Ty dismounted by the house tie-rail under the cottonwoods and headed for the kitchen door. Out of his town suit and dressed in his working range clothes, he cut an absurd figure and he knew it. He was much more comfortable in congress gaiters than cowman's boots. His levis were too tight for him and the waistband cut into his soft, overhanging belly. His gloves protected white, fleshy hands that had never known a rope burn and his sand-colored Stetson was heavier and hotter than his panama. Still, a man who was a rancher had to dress like one, even down to the buttonless vest over a calico shirt.

As he tramped past the front door, angling

toward the kitchen wing, he saw that Callie was doing her washing. The tub and rinse tub were outside on a bench, reasonably handy to the hot water on the inside stove. Her knuckles, muffled by clothes as she scrubbed, made such a racket on the washboard that she didn't hear him approach. He halted a little way from her and regarded her curiously. She was working in a quiet, sustained fury, like a man would work at chopping wood harmlessly to vent his anger. Her dress front and apron were wet from splashed water and her red hair was dishevelled and sparkling in the sun. She straightened up now, wiping the perspiration from her forehead with her forearm and only then saw her father watching her. "Why, Pa, how long have you been standing there?" she asked.

"Not long. It's always nice to see somebody else working." He came up to her and gave her a gentle, sideways hug of affection. "Let's talk for a minute, Callie."

"All right, but out here, Pa. The kitchen's a furnace." She gestured to a pair of chairs, one a battered rocking chair, under the nearest cottonwood which they often used to escape the summer heat of the house. "You sit down. I've got some coffee on the stove."

Ty moved over and sat down on the

weathered rocker and presently Callie came out with two tin cups of coffee and joined him. Here in the shade the soft wind that rustled the leaves overhead was pleasant and cool. When Callie had seated herself on the straight chair, Ty put his cup on the ground beside his chair to let it cool and said, "That trial put everybody back a week's work. Reese too, I reckon."

"Yes, he was up ahead of me, Pa. They're building a new line camp and corral at Lime Canyon. He'll be gone a week maybe."

"Did you talk to him last night late?" Callie frowned. "No. Why? What's happened?"

Ty took a cautious sip of his coffee, found the temperature right, took two swallows, then wiped the coffee off his already stained moustaches with his free hand. "Nothing much. He threw Buddy, June, Emmett and Big John into jail last night. As far as he's concerned," he added wryly, "there's nothing too good for the Hoads."

"What for?" Callie asked.

"Oh, they were drinking a little, making some noise. Jim Daley thought Buddy was kind of loud and tried to take him in. The boys wouldn't let him and some shooting started. Reese heard it and came over to break it up. He knocked Big John cold and then he made Buddy and the other two boys lug Big John to jail. He locked them all up overnight. Like I say, there's nothing too good for us Hoads." He was watching Callie's face and saw it flush with anger.

"He's dead set against us, Pa. I don't know why, but he just is. I'm a good wife to him, but I don't think he even likes me."

"Come back home if you want, Callie. You know you're always welcome."

Callie shook her head shortly. "I can't, Pa. He did me a good turn, the best a man can do."

"Does he give you money, Callie?" Ty asked with seeming irrelevance.

Callie shrugged. "Enough. I've never been used to much anyway. You know that." Then the oddity of his question struck her. "Why d'you ask that, Pa?"

Ty finished off his coffee, then leaned back in his chair. "Well, Orv and me had an idea on how to make all us Hoads some money, pretty big money too. That includes you, Callie. Fact is we can't make it without your help."

"My help?" Callie asked. "What can I do that somebody else can't do better?"

Matter of factly then Ty told her of the scheme. They would raid the herds on the National Trail, hide the beef in Copper Canyon and sell them through a cattle company of which she would be the president. Ty finished by saying, "We'll only be stealing from thieves, Callie. Them Texans stole the cattle originally from their neighbors, so stealing from them don't really mean stealing."

Callie nodded. "But why me, Pa? Any one of you knows more about buying and selling cattle than I could learn in fifty years."

"No, it has to be you, Callie. You have to sign all our bills of sale or the scheme won't work."

Callie frowned. "I don't understand, Pa. Why couldn't you or Uncle Orv or even Buddy sign them?"

Ty leaned forward now with elbows on knees. "Because you're married to Reese Branham, Sheriff of Sutton County. If he catches us, he'll have to prosecute the company. That'll be you. Like a wife can't testify against her husband, a husband can't testify against his wife. Now d'you see?"

Callie was silent, staring past her father as she pondered this. Then a ghost of a smile touched her thin lips. "You mean him still being Sheriff couldn't do anything to me?"

"The law says he can't testify against you, just like you can't testify against him," Ty repeated.

"Lordy," Callie breathed softly.

Ty didn't push it. He waited, watching her, trying to read the fleeting emotions that crossed her face. Finally she said, "He won't like it, Pa."

"What d'you care? He don't even like you, you said."

"No," Callie said softly, remembering.

"You can wind up kind of rich and independent as a hog on ice. It'll be your money, Callie, to buy your dresses to wear on your trips to the places you want to go." He gestured toward her tubs. "You can pay for somebody even to wash for you."

"That's not only why I'd do it, Pa," Callie said quietly. "It's getting even that I'd like. He thinks us Hoads are trash. I wonder if he'd think a rich Hoad was trash."

"Why, the rich are never trash, honey. Only the poor like us are trash."

Callie nodded. "I'll do it, Pa. Now go through it all again. Slow."

Ty did, answering all Callie's questions. Afterwards he told her that now she was willing to front for the Hoad Land & Cattle Company, he was on his way to Bale to see the lawyer, Martin Farmer, who had defended Orville. Farmer would draw up the papers of incorporation for her to sign. She would probably get them tomorrow and then Farmer would file them with the county clerk. Orville, June and Buddy would come to his house tonight and a list of the Hoad relations would be drawn up to be approached and asked to join. They would do that tomorrow while Big John and Emmett would head for the National Trail to find out what herds were moving up to it. It was easy enough to learn that because every trail boss and his hands knew whose herds had started ahead of him and whose were following him, since the herds were mostly made up at the same few Texas communities. Now he had to get on, Ty said, for there was much to do.

Callie walked him over to his horse and then returned, not to her washing, but to the battered rocking chair her father had just vacated. She wanted to think more about this since she knew instinctively this was the turning point in her married life.

Just what did she stand to lose by heading up this band? Almost nothing, she thought with a bitter candor. She was unloved, married to a stranger, childless and lonely and with no prospect of any of this ever changing to something else or for the better. She was not physically afraid of Reese because he was gentle with women, all women.

If that was all she stood to lose, what did she stand to gain? Well, money for one thing. She and Buddy had never suffered from want of enough to eat and wear. In spite of his poor-mouthing, her father had always earned a fair living back in Tennessee, trading, buying and selling stock or anything that could be moved, leaving their mother to take care of them and force their schooling and teach them pride. But still Callie had always had a hunger for physical possessions, the things she could feel and touch and look at and say to herself, "This is mine and mine alone." It could be anything — a dress, a carved mirror, a pretty little mare or a man. She supposed this same craving for possessions was what drove most women into harlotry, but that didn't make it any the less real. She would like to be rich enough so that if she saw a woman in the street whose dress she admired, she could stop her and say, "I'll buy that"; or if she saw one of those beautiful, delicate buggies, with red-painted wheels as fragile as lace, she would like to be able to say, "It's got to be mine. I'll pay you whatever you ask." Admittedly, Callie believed that possessions made people and that without them people weren't worth bothering much about. If one day she could appear before Reese in a rich dress with real jewels, would he love her again? She doubted that, but she knew one thing, he would place some value on her. All those preachers' admonitions to shun material things, that money is the root of all evil, that it was impossible for a rich man to get into heaven were just so much nonsense dreamed up by poor people for poor people. Why care if you couldn't get into heaven if you had heaven on earth?

Callie rose, suddenly feeling that this was a new kind of a day now. The Hoads, with herself heading them, would finally come into their own.

Exactly a week after Reese left the Slash Seven, he stood beside his foreman in the morning sunlight and both regarded the new line shack. It stood at the edge of a broad park high in the Wheeler range, whose foothills stretched down almost to the outskirts of Bale. Surrounding the big park that was already dotted with Slash Seven cattle were the towering spruce from which the line shack had been built. Its freshly peeled logs were yellow-pink in the morning sun and the ground around the new three-room building was littered with long strips of peeled bark. The new building abutted the old line shack and was three times its size. The smell of sun-warmed pitch was everywhere around it, inside and out.

"Well, there it is, even if it damn near killed us all," Reese said.

Ames Tolliver was a dozen years older than Reese and built like a bank vault. Any shirt he bought was torn at the forearms and biceps after a day's wear, so it was his custom to saw off the shirtsleeves above the elbow to give his huge arms room to move. His face was square and homely, topped by iron-rimmed spectacles, which he had to wear if he wanted to move safely in an area as small as a room. The lenses magnified his blue eyes hugely so that he always seemed to wear a startled look. His range clothes were worn and smeared with pine pitch as were Reese's.

"It's too pretty to call a line shack, Reese. Too big, too."

"It beats a tent," Reese conceded. He looked down at his blistered and pitch-stained hands. The five of them had worked like fools this past week, cutting, hauling and splitting logs and shingles and digging post holes for the new corral across and down the creek. Glancing that way, Reese saw Sam Commery, the youngest crew member, heading up toward them afoot, driving a harnessed team. He was, Reese knew, heading for the loaded wagon by the old line shack that held their tools. Looking again at the house in quiet approval, Reese wondered again why he or his father years ago had not enlarged the single room shack. This high country was really

Slash Seven's main house when the hot summer winds began to burn the lower range. It was cool here and the grass was plentiful and now, thanks to the new building, it would be habitable for the crew and for Callie and himself.

"We forgot something, Ames," Reese said and he cut in front of his foreman, heading for the wagon. Standing between the wheels of its left side, he opened the big tool box and lifted out a hammer and some nails. From a keg in the wagon he lifted out a new horseshoe and then tramped over to the door of the new building. While Ames moved up to watch him, Reese nailed the shoe solidly to the lintel log above the door, wincing a little at each blow. He looked at his hands now and said, "Even that hurts."

He moved back to put away the hammer, then headed for the corral, crossing the double-log footbridge ahead of Ames. This had been a pleasant, if driving, week, Reese thought. They had worked from sun-up till long past dark, at first sleeping with the sky above them, then with walls around them, then with a roof over them, and the work after the long days in court was the purest kind of joy.

They passed Sam who was limping a little. He grinned at Reese and said, "I'm going to

61

drive back lying face down on the blanket rolls. I'm too sore to sit down."

"Just don't go to sleep," Reese said.

At the corral they caught their horses and saddled them. Steve Ashton and Walt Ryder, the other two hands, had saddled up and were halfway across the park by now. When Reese's grey was saddled, he watched Ames close the gate, then they rode off across the grassy park, headed for Bale and the Slash Seven.

When Reese and Ames caught up with the other two, Steve and Walt were already discussing how it would feel to drown in the Best Bet's beer. Steve was the younger, in his twenties, a lean, long-faced young man with a smouldering insolence in his eyes that never found its way to his speech. He was cynical, yet almost courtly in his manner, and women of a certain type found him irresistible. Walt Ryder was a taciturn, ruddy-faced Scotsman who had been imported by one of the big English owned ranches up north. A quarrel with the owners which he would never discuss had set him adrift to be hired by Reese's father. In his fifties, he would long since have been foreman if he had not shunned all the responsibilities that Ames Tolliver was willing to accept.

The wagon road, such as it was, snaked through the dark timber, and Reese paid little attention to the slow-paced talk of his crew. He had started the morning with a carefree sense of satisfaction at having accomplished some hard and necessary work, but as they approached the pinyon-clad foothills above Bale, his feeling of well being slowly wore off to be replaced by a vague depression. At the end of his ride today Callie would be waiting for him — a silent, rebellious and bewildered Callie with whom he had no communication whatsoever.

Reese dropped off the crew at the Best Bet, then turned off Main Street, heading for the court-house. Out in the distant prairie a storm was drifting in. He wondered what had come up during this past week that Jim Daley had had to handle. There couldn't have been anything serious for Jim would have sent for him, he knew.

Putting his horse in under the open-faced shed behind the court-house, he tramped up the court-house steps and entered the rear door of the corridor. He found his office was locked, which meant that Jim Daley was out on an errand. Since he carried no keys with him, he would either have to wait for Jim's return or query one of the court-house officials on what had happened in his absence. Then he thought of Jen who, though she seldom used her father's office, might be there today.

He climbed the stairs to the second floor and turned left toward the Judge's chambers next to the court-room. The door adjoining the Judge's chambers was open and Reese felt a sudden rush of pleasure knowing that Jen was here.

Tramping into the room which held a small conference table and chairs plus the desk and files, he saw Jen seated in the swivel chair that she had pulled up to the low window. Her feet were on the windowsill and she seemed to be looking out over the summer-lazy town.

At his entrance she turned her head and smiled. "I saw you ride in, Reese, and hoped you'd come up."

She was wearing a grey-colored, lightweight summer dress with a touch of white on the collar and on the cuffs of the short sleeves, a dress Reese remembered and liked.

"I had to find out if the court-house had burned down. Tell me what's been happening." He came over to the big window, leaned down and gently shifted her legs so he could sit down on the sill facing her. She smiled lazily and affectionately.

"The same old nothing," Jen said. "I came down to make a pass at working, but when I looked out the window, I saw that storm shaping up. I've been watching it."

Reese nodded. "We'll be getting it at home but not near here, looks like."

"What've you got all over your hands and clothes?" Jen asked.

"Pitch from logs for the new line shack," Reese answered. Then he asked, "How's your father?"

Jen hesitated a moment. "Puzzled, I'd guess you'd call it, or maybe surprised."

"At what?"

"At some gossip I picked up from the county clerk today." She paused. "Reese, why is Callie going into the cattle and land business?"

Reese felt a shock he tried to hide and couldn't. "I didn't know she was."

"Martin Farmer filed the incorporation papers of the Hoad Land & Cattle Company this morning. Callie's named as president of it."

Reese shook his head in bewilderment. "That happened while I was gone." He smiled faintly. "She doesn't own any land and hasn't got a cow to call her own." He paused, then asked, "Who are the other officers?"

"Martin Farmer is secretary. The names of the president and secretary are all that the State requires, although most companies list all officers. That's what puzzled Dad and me. And now you too, I suppose."

Reese rubbed his jaw in thought and the

gesture made a faint rasping sound on his week's dark beard-stubble. "Well, her father's been a trader of sorts all his life — all kinds of stock or anything he could swap for. Sounds like it might be Ty's idea."

Jen nodded. "That's probably it."

"But why Callie's named president I can't guess. Maybe he did it to humor her."

Jen smiled. "Everybody should be president of something in a lifetime. I was president of my fifth grade class. As I recall it, it was very satisfying to my little ego."

Reese grinned. "You probably let the boys kiss you if they'd vote for you."

Now Jen laughed. "No, it wasn't that complicated. All the boys were monsters but there were more girls than boys. I just organized the girls."

Reese knew they were both talking just to be talking about anything but Jen's strange news of Callie. Certainly this was the oddest way any husband ever learned that his wife had launched into a business venture. Was it a result of their last quarrel or had she been planning it all along? He felt a new restlessness now and it was touched with irritation. He hated to be surprised by plans that he should have known at their inception, and now he rose.

"Jim got any problems?"

Jen shook her head. "The jail's empty, and Jim might even be fishing."

Reese bid her an abrupt goodbye, tramped downstairs and outside to his horse. Mounting him, he put him directly through town, knowing as he passed the Best Bet that his crew was still there.

He took the short cut across the prairie toward the Slash Seven and felt the chill ground breeze, which preceded the coming storm. He paused long enough to untie his slicker and don it and then saw that the rain had already blacked out the distant trees at home. The same questions kept troubling him now. Should he challenge Callie immediately, demanding to know what she planned and why she planned it? No matter what their relationship, she was his wife and he had a right to know of her activities. But would she tell him any more than he already knew? It came to him then that demanding an explanation of her might be precisely the wrong way to find out what she was up to. Why not pretend ignorance and let events develop as they would? After all, it was only through chance and then curiosity that Jen had learned of the new corporation. The few people who would learn of it would think it was Reese's idea and that it was his whim to make his wife president. If he didn't bring it up to Callie, then she would assume that he knew nothing about it or that he was so indifferent to her and her doings that he didn't care.

The first few drops of rain quickly turned into a slashing downpour as the storm rode over him. Yes, that was what he could do, he thought then — say nothing and watch, say nothing and wait.

When he rode in to the Slash Seven, it was raining in great driving sheets; the bare barn lot seemed to boil with the rain that hit the hard ground and, now muddy, bounced up a foot before settling again.

Reese put his grey in the open-faced stable, rubbing him down with a gunny sack, then headed through the driving rain for the kitchen door to the house. The usual smoke from the stove was missing, Reese noted, or else the battering rain had beat it down.

He stepped through the kitchen doorway and closed it behind him and looked about the room which was empty. He stood there, water channelling down his slicker around his boots and called, "Callie."

There was no answer and only then did he notice the piece of paper on the kitchen table held down by a salt cellar. Moving over to it, he picked it up and saw that it was in Callie's nervous handwriting. The note read, "You had your week. Now I'll have mine. Callie."

2

Big John's message, brought home to Orville by Emmett, was that there was a herd of two thousand Texas cattle on its way up the National Trail and that it would be in the vicinity of the Little Muddy in three days. The message came four days after Reese started work on the line shack and Ty immediately came over to Slash Seven with a wagonload of grub, picked Callie up and then headed for Ty's line shack in Copper Canyon to get the Hoad camp in readiness.

Orville Hoad was ready and had his organization planned, his men primed to go when the message arrived. Buddy, Ty's boy, would pick up the two young Plunkets, Abner and Marvin, who were the sons of Sarah Plunket, sister to Orville and Ty. Another sister, Amy Bashear, had three boys, grown and married men, who had agreed to make up a second unit. The third, of course, would be Orv with Emmett, Junior and Big John.

Nine men traveling together would attract attention and be remembered, Orville knew, so he directed the units to travel separately to their rendezvous with Big John at the Little

Muddy. Here they would learn from Big John the location of the herd and agree on the date and time for stampeding it. Afterwards they would split up again and once they had stampeded the herd they would make their gather separately and take different routes to Ty's Copper Canyon line shack. Orville had cautioned them not to be greedy; the more cattle they had to drive, the slower the pace would be. The idea was to strike swiftly and get out in a hurry. If the stampede succeeded, the drover and his trail crew would have to spend days rounding up the herd and counting it, and by that time the cattle should be well through the rough badlands country that covered twenty of the forty miles between Bale and the National Trail. Even after they reached the Wheelers they must approach Copper Canyon by different routes.

The night the three units rendezvoused at Big John's camp, it was raining and Orville learned from his eldest son that the herd was bedded down less than five miles down the Trail. The three units set off immediately, separating. Orville would fire the first shots that would start the stampede an hour before dawn. It was unlikely that the trail crew could start the cattle milling since they already would be wet, miserable and spooky. They would, Orville hoped, stampede west into the broken country before the brakes, which would make the job of rounding them up twice as difficult as if they were stampeded up the Trail.

The plan worked to perfection; the trail crew was double-guarding the restless herd, but Orville's shots simply turned the storm-caused uneasiness of the cattle into instant panic. His shots drew a return fire from the night herders that only increased the panic and, since Orville's station was on the east side of the herd, the cattle ran west as Orville hoped they would. The attempt to turn the herd and get them to mill in a circle failed and the herd running west spread out where the other two units started their roundup of the lead cattle before the trail crew on their weary horses could begin their search for the scattered bunches of cattle.

The rain held on all that day, alternating between a drizzle and occasional downpours that, Orville knew, would erase all tracks. He and his boys had sixty head in their band as they headed into the brakes in mid-morning. Whatever trails they left around the rocks at the base of the clay dunes and canyon floors were erased by the rain. By afternoon they were on the range that held other cattle whose tracks and signs would confuse any possible pursuit.

By the third day after the stampede the three units had arrived at Ty's line cabin. Together they had got away with one hundred and ninety-eight double-wintered Texas beeves. Ty's log line shack consisted of a single room fronted by an open park where the men immediately set about vent-branding the cattle and re-branding them with the HL connected brand which was already registered as the brand of the Hoad Land & Cattle Company. During these days the eleven men of the Hoad blood line slept in two dirty grey tents pitched back of the line shack. Callie cooked and served the meals and slept alone in the line shack. She worked as hard as any of the men and each night before darkness set in she would look out across the big meadow at their newly acquired wealth and a renewed determination mixed with pride came to her. Big John, while waiting, had learned the name of the approaching herd's owner, so that Callie could forge a bill of sale with the name of the Texas owner. If by some unlikely chance anyone strayed into the remote Copper Canyon and was curious, the bill of sale would be ready for him.

This day, the branding finished, the Plunkets and the Bashears and two of Orville's boys and Buddy had left for home, leaving Ty, Orville and Big John in camp with Callie.

That evening after supper Orville lighted the lantern and hung it on a piece of baling wire over the big deal table.

Callie, dressed in levis and a man's shirt, distributed the four tin cups, two on each side of the table before the saw log stools. She poured the coffee, then watched the three men move toward their seats.

Her father, who had done little these past few days save rustle wood for the branding fire, sat down first as befitted the patriarch of the Hoad clan. His working clothes still retained an unsoiled, store-bought newness about them. Orville, however, was dirty and unshaven and he smelled, but his lean beard-stubbled face and his hawk nose and his arrogant pale eyes held an authority that her father's face entirely lacked. He, Callie knew, was the driving force in the family, the one who held it together in prideful cohesiveness. He had the guile, the gentleness to his own blood and the disdain for all other men which all the Hoads admired and copied.

Big John was the last to be seated, a man so huge that sitting down he was almost as tall as Callie standing. He had his father's blade of a nose and his mother's straight hair, black as any Indian's. His heavy face held the innocent benignity of an almost simple-minded child but, remembering his boyhood fights with her brother Buddy, Callie knew that he was as savage as any panther when temper took him. He too was dirty and unshaven and so much in need of a haircut that his hat, which he now took off, rode his mop of Indian hair like a woman's bonnet.

Orville looked at him and grinned, revealing his sharp, tobacco-stained teeth. He shifted a cud of plug tobacco into his other cheek, spat on the floor and said, "My God, Big John. Get Callie to cut your hair tonight before she leaves tomorrow. Another week and you won't be able to get a hat on."

"I didn't bring scissors or clippers, Uncle Orville."

"Well, take my hunting knife like I used to take on him when he was a kid."

Callie nodded and came over and sat down.

"Callie," Orville began. "What you going to tell Reese where you've been?"

"Visiting Aunt Amy," Callie said. "We'll stop by on the way home and fix the story with her."

Orville nodded and looked at his son. "Big John, I don't reckon anybody will stop by here while you're alone. If they do, treat them good. They get nosey about the cattle, just say it's the first bunch bought up in Texas by the Hoad Land & Cattle Company. You don't know where they come from, you're just working for wages for your cousin Callie."

Orville turned his head and spat again. "Callie, ain't no sense in telling Reese about these cattle. If he finds out, tell him the Bashear boys traded for them in Texas. Tell him they come cheap because they was Government bought beef headed for an Indian reservation. The agent sold them to the Bashears and kept the money. He was going to blame his short count on a Canadian river flash flood that caught his herd by surprise. You got the bill of sale and you got the Bashear boys to back up the story."

"Amy's boys was always good traders. Reese know that," Ty said.

Orville nodded. "Callie, you'll be the first to know if Reese hears about that stampede on the National."

"I don't reckon," Callie contradicted. "He won't tell me anything."

"Still, keep your ears open. Like I told all the boys, soon's we can move these cattle, me and my boys will drive them over into Moffitt County. After I sell, I'll open an account in the bank at Moffitt. No use letting the bank here know how much money we're making." Now he pushed himself to his feet. "Me, I'm hitting the blankets." He drew his hunting knife from his sheath and tossed it on the table in front of Callie. "Get to work on Big John,

75

Callie. Just go careful around the ears. They're so damn big, they're hard to miss."

Reese was doing some hated bookwork in his court-house office that morning when he became certain that he was being watched. When he turned his head he saw a man almost as big as himself standing silently in the doorway. The stranger wore ancient chaps over his work-worn levis, his half-boots had dried mud on them and his buttonless vest was as weather-faded as his shirt and battered Stetson. He seemed a man in his middle thirties whose lean and homely face hadn't seen a razor in weeks. His nose, once broken, was badly mended and this fact, together with his bold and friendly blue eyes, gave an observer a feeling that he had fought much and would fight much more and was not especially concerned with the odds against him.

"You're Sheriff Branham and I'm Will Reston. Want a little parley with you."

Reese gestured toward the chair and Reston, unmistakably a Texan, tramped across the room and slacked into the chair. He made no effort to shake hands.

"What can I do for you?" Reese asked quietly.

"Don't rightly know yet." He looked around the room and his glance halted on a wall map. He rose now, saying, "Let's start with this here map now. Would you kindly look at it with me."

Reese rose and joined him at the map which was of Sutton County. Reston raised a finger and placed it roughly four inches off the right-hand side of the map and said, "The National would be about here, d'you reckon?" When Reese nodded, Reston went on moving his finger an inch up the wall. "The Little Muddy would be about here, looks like."

Reese now touched the map and said, "The head waters start in the brakes here."

"Well, I come to the right place then," Reston said mildly. He turned and went back to his chair. Reese came back and sat down and now Reston with a stiff thumb pushed his hat up off his forehead. "Four, five days — no — nights ago my herd was stampeded off the National."

"Lightning?" Reese asked.

"No, sir, gunfire. One of my night herders was stomped to doll rags. The herd was scattered for fifteen miles."

"The National doesn't cross Sutton County, Reston."

"I know that, but the herd was stampeded toward your county, right at the brakes."

"And you're missing some beef, I take it."

"We lost a couple of dozen killed but that

don't add up to over two hundred."

"Can you give me anything to go on?" Reese asked. "See anybody? Hear 'em talk?"

"No. Only thing I can give you to go on is my brand. R-Cross on the left hip."

"And you think they're in Sutton County?"

"All I know is that they were headed this way," Reston said. "It rained the whole damn day and night too and a stolen cow makes the same tracks as a cow that ain't stolen. When we finally run into stuff with local brands, we quit looking."

Reese nodded. "What do you want me to do, Reston?"

"I don't know your people and you do," Reston said mildly. "You lost much stock here?"

"Once in a while we run across a fresh hide. We figure it's likely some miner from one of the mines up in the Wheelers is too lazy to hunt his own buckskin. Nobody misses many cattle, so there's your answer. Folks around here are average honest, maybe better than average."

"Many herds on the National raided?"

"You'd know more about that than I would, being a drover," Reese answered. "I understand they had some trouble but that was further south and the trouble was Indian."

Reston grunted. "Still is." Now he put his

78

hands on his knees, about to rise. "Don't reckon I give you much to go on, but, damn! I hate a thief." He pushed himself erect now and said, "If any of my stuff shows up, just write me at Big Island, Texas."

Reese rose and they shook hands. After Reston had gone Reese wrote down his name, address and brand on a slip of paper which he tucked in one of the desk pigeon holes. Then, leaning back in his chair, he looked out the window. If Reston was right, this was disturbing news — but was he right? Reese had heard of stampedes where a third of the stampeded herd had simply vanished. Some drovers would accept a two hundred head loss as one of the accepted hazards met along the hundred miles of trail, but apparently Reston wasn't one of them. With nothing more than Reston's story to go on, there was little he himself could do except look out for R-Cross branded cattle. That number wouldn't be easy to hide. If they were here, they would show. It was a worrisome thing too, Reese thought. When a county got a bad name with drovers, it could mean real trouble. An angry trail crew could wreck a town if it thought the town was in league against it.

The only thing he could do was wait and then he thought wryly, *I'm getting pretty good at that.*

★ ★ ★

It was Buddy Hoad who first spotted the R-Cross branded bay pony at the Best Bet tie-rail and the shock of seeing it stopped him cold in his tracks on the boardwalk. This was the brand he and the other Hoads had just got through venting on two hundred stolen cattle. Now it appeared on the left hip of a rangy bay tied in front of the Bale saloon and Buddy felt a moment of panic. He looked at the horses racked on either side of the bay and saw with a vast relief that the other horses had local brands, which meant that the bay's owner was probably alone.

Buddy's next move was instinctive. He turned and retraced his steps past the blacksmith's shop and Silberman's Emporium and shouldered his way through the batwing doors of Macey's Saloon, where he had left his Uncle Orville only a minute ago. Macey's was a small saloon and shabby, with a bar on the left. Tim Macey had married one of Amy Bashear's daughters, so he was counted a Hoad. Bald and short, a soft and surly man of forty, he was now filling pint bottles from a gallon jug behind the bar. Orville was giving him a lazy attention and Buddy moved in beside him. "Uncle Orv, you better come with me," Buddy said quietly.

Something in Buddy's voice made Orville

look at him abruptly. "All right," Orville said mildly.

He followed Buddy out of the saloon and caught up with him as they passed the blacksmith's shop.

"See that bay past the break in the tie-rail?"

"What about him?"

"Look at his brand."

The two men moved and when Orville saw the brand, he, like Buddy had before him, halted abruptly. "Well now," he said softly, swivelling his glance from the horse to the Best Bet's half doors. Without speaking to Buddy, he pushed into the saloon bar just inside the door. The big room held a couple of men drinking at one of the card tables and a half dozen at the bar full down its length. Orville knew every man in the room and now he traveled half the length of the bar, Buddy trailing him. He halted. The bartender left his other customers and came up to them. He was a bony man, red-eyed from drink, and his white apron at this hour of the morning was still unsoiled.

"Perry, see that bay out at the break in the tie-rail?"

Perry leaned over so he could see beyond the open bat-wings. "Yeah," he said then. "Looks like he's forgot to eat."

"Who owns him?" Orville asked.

Perry straightened up. "Some Texas trail

hand. He come in earlier, asked the sheriff's name, bought himself a drink, then headed for the court-house."

"Did he now?" Orville said softly.

He turned and went out and again Buddy trailed him. Pausing on the boardwalk just to the right of the door, Orville half sat down on the sill of the many-paned window. Slowly, almost thoughtfully, he stroked the ridge of his narrow, hawk nose. Finally, Buddy watching had to speak. "What d'you think, Uncle Orv?"

"I think we're in trouble, Buddy, but I don't know what kind of trouble."

"If he seen any of us or had anything Reese could use, Reese would be on to us right now."

"Maybe not. Maybe Reese would wait until he got the goods on us. But us, we can't wait."

A look of exasperation emphasized the arrogance in Buddy's face. "What d'you mean, we can't wait? We got to wait, don't we? We don't walk up to Reese and say, 'You looking for us?' "

"We can't wait," Orville repeated. "In half an hour or so this R-Cross rider will be heading back to catch up with his herd on the National. Or, even worse, he could start snooping."

"What you trying to tell me, Uncle Orv?"

Orville looked up at him, his pale eyes

bright with anger. "I don't rightly know myself," he said flatly. "We ain't got the time to call everybody together. We got maybe a half hour like I said to figure what we do about this R-Cross rider."

"But what *can* we do?" Buddy asked, the exasperation still in his voice.

"You figure it out," Orville said harshly. "I just got out of a court-room. I don't aim to get in it again and have a witness say, 'Yes, that's the man, that's his voice, that's his looks.' "

"But you ain't sure he saw us or could identify us," Buddy protested.

"You want to take a chance he didn't?" Orville asked softly.

"But ain't he already told Reese all he knows?"

"If he hadn't been a witness to something, he wouldn't be here, would he?"

Buddy had no answer to that and he watched his uncle carefully. If Uncle Orville said they couldn't let this go, that meant just one thing and he didn't like to think about it. Finally, Buddy said one word, a question. "Here?"

"No, not here."

"How?"

"We'll see." They heard footsteps on the plankwalk at the far corner of the Best Bet, and Orville slowly turned his head. A tall man in rough range clothes was approaching them. He passed them, heading for the R-Cross branded bay. Now, Orville pushed himself to his feet and walked over to the break in the tie-rail and moved into the street just as Reston stepped into his saddle.

"Been waiting for you," Orville said pleasantly. "Saw your R-Cross brand."

Reston lowered his hands, crossed them on the saddle horn and looked down at this lanky, pale-eyed stranger. His glance shifted to Buddy and seeing the family resemblance, he assumed this was a son. Neither of them looked truculent, but they did look curious.

"It's a Texas brand," Reston said.

Orville nodded. "Seen it before."

Reston regarded him carefully. "Now that ain't likely, but where did you see it?"

"I got a place over east, borderin' the brakes. Me and my boy got a cow outfit over there. Yesterday — no, day before it was — I seen some R-Cross branded steers mixed with mine. It ain't a local brand and I couldn't figure it out. Then I seen your brand just now and figured I'd wait and tell you."

"That's mighty kind of you," Reston said. "How many steers of mine did you see?"

"I seen three," Orville said. He looked over his shoulder at Buddy. "How many'd you count, Buddy, after I left you?"

"Only two more."

"How do I find your place?" Reston asked.

"Well, it ain't easy," Orville said. He thought a moment, "Tell you what. Me and Buddy got a few fool errands to do, then I got to pick up a horse other side of town. Why don't we meet you at the bridge in half an hour and we'll show you where we seen 'em."

"If it ain't out of your way, I'd appreciate that," Reston said. "Half an hour at the bridge."

Orville nodded and turned. "Well, Buddy, come along and we'll get our buyin' done."

Reston sat motionless a moment, watching the two men tramp down the boardwalk. This was certainly a friendly act, he thought, especially to a stranger. If the older man had identified his horse's brand, he needed only to keep his mouth shut to gain five double-wintered steers. What was it that the Sheriff had said? These were average people here, better than average maybe. Well, he'd have to agree with that, Reston thought.

True to his word Reston was waiting at the bridge over Lime Creek when Orville and Buddy arrived a half hour later. The three set out east toward the distant brakes.

Orville, whose small outfit lay to the south,

had set the appointment at the bridge because he didn't want to be seen in company with Reston. Staying clear of the stage road and the few wagon roads leading to ranches, they rode steadily for four hours. In that time, by careful circumlocution, Orville learned that Reston, during the half hour wait after their meeting, had not been curious enough about them to ask anyone their names. Now that he was sure that Reston hadn't discussed them with anyone in town, Orville finally introduced himself and Buddy. Presently, Reston was talking about the stampede. Orville listened with sympathetic interest as Reston told of his conviction that some of his cattle had been stolen and that they were either in Sutton County or had been driven through it. Orville asked him then with only the mildest curiosity if he had any notion of who composed the gang that had caused the stampede. Reston didn't answer immediately, wondering what he should say. If these Hoads, friendly as they were, took back the word that cattle thieves had got clean away with his cattle, it would encourage further raids in the future. Why, then, not pretend that he did have some information which he was in the process of tracking down.

Accordingly, he said in answer to Orville's question, "Why, yes. One of my men got thrown in the stampede and stomped some. He can take care of himself but he was too crippled up to head up the trail right away. He heard names and saw a man by lightning flash that he'd recognize if he saw him again." He paused. Then to underline his point, he added, "Soon's he can ride, I'm going to bring him over to talk with your Sheriff Branham."

"He got water over there where you left him?"

"Oh yes, he's on the Little Muddy."

Orville looked obliquely at Buddy who was already looking at him. Any lingering doubts as to the wisdom of what he was going to do died in Orville then.

They saw occasional clusters of cattle as they approached the brakes, great clay and rock dunes that held the poorest graze on the floors of its canyon.

Orville raised his arm and pointed. "There's an old mine road that short cuts to my place back in the brakes. We'll take that."

They headed into the narrow canyon, Orville in the lead. Around a couple of bends of canyon bottom the walls fell back. Ahead of them on the canyon floor lay an abandoned log cabin, its roof fallen in. Up the side of the canyon was a great dune of tailings which almost hid the sagging head frame of a mine shaft. When they were even with the cabin,

Orville reined in and Reston came up on his right. Orville had shifted his reins to his left hand and now, holding the reins, he lifted his arm across his body in a pointing gesture. "To look at it, you'd never think a half million dollars come out of that hole, would you?"

Reston turned his head to look up at the mine. He heard too late the whisper of a gun barrel on leather. Reston's hand was driving for his own gun, his head half-turned, when Orville shot. At a distance of five feet he could scarcely miss and he didn't. The thud of the slug caught Reston in his side just below the shoulder, and the force of it drove him out of the saddle on to the neck of Buddy's horse. Reston's horse, terrified by the explosion, began plunging and bucking as Reston himself fell heavily to the ground, dead before he hit it.

Suddenly then, Reston's horse, free of its burden, started to run up the canyon. Cursing, Orville raised his gun and emptied it at the rangy bay. Buddy belatedly joined in the fusillade and then, apparently untouched, the horse galloped out of sight around a bend.

Buddy spurred his own mount in pursuit and Orville called sharply, "Come back! Buddy, come back!"

Buddy checked his horse, turned it and came back to rein in by his uncle. Orville didn't even look at Reston as he asked dryly, "You aim to make me tow him up that hill alone?"

"We got to get that damn horse, Uncle Orville."

"Let him run hisself out. There ain't no place he can go."

Orville stepped out of the saddle, moved up to Reston and toed him over on his back. Reston's eyes were open but sightless and already the blood flowing out of the wound was attracting flies.

Orville stepped over, picked up Reston's hat and carefully placed it on Reston's right boot which was pointing skyward.

"You take his feet," Orville said.

Together, wordlessly, with Orville at the head and Buddy at the feet, they carried Reston's body up the sloping talus of tailings. At the summit they could look down a short slope which ended in a square mine shaft whose timber cribbing was already rotting. Carefully, heels digging in, they moved the body close to the shaft, then dumped it on the shaft edge. Reston's body rolled over, hesitated on the brink and then the top timber gave way. Reston's body followed it into the black, lightless hole. They heard the body thudding against the cribbing a half dozen times, then there was silence for a moment, then a dim, almost inaudible thud came to them.

Now Orville looked at Buddy, whose face was pale and held a residue of a fear that was almost panic. Abruptly then, Buddy turned and began to vomit, and Orville watched him with silent contempt. Almost indifferently he began to climb up to the top of the tailings, heedless of Buddy's retchings. At the top Orville halted and was presently joined by Buddy.

"Pity you had to do that," Orville said. "Because you ain't going to eat for some little while."

"How you figure that?" Buddy asked miserably.

"First we get his horse, then we head for the Little Muddy to get his friend. That'll be tomorrow sometime."

Reese's hated paperwork which Reston had interrupted yesterday and which was resumed today was an estimate of expenses incurred in tracking down Shep, the surprise witness in Orville Hoad's trial. It consisted of meals, the cost of which he hadn't kept track of, putting up his horse at several feed stables, uncounted drinks he had bought the witness, the cost of Shep's journey to testify and Shep's board and room that Shep couldn't remember.

It all amounted to a larger sum than Reese had anticipated, but he could find no flaw in his addition. It occurred to him then that Jen, who had worked with him in finding Shep, had known his every move and could judge whether the bill which would be submitted to the commissioners was not only reasonable but accurate.

On the off chance that Jen might be in her father's office, he rose, headed down the corridor and climbed the stairs. Again he found the door to the district attorney's office open and when he walked into the room, he found Jen standing on a chair to reach the top row of an eight foot rack of pigeon holes which served as an auxiliary file.

When she turned to see who had come in she lost her balance, caught herself a little late, then jumped lightly to the floor.

"Your curiosity will get you a broken neck some day," Reese said.

"Well, nobody ever comes in here, and when they do, it's an occasion," Jen said. She wore a yellow, half-sleeved summer dress of calico which, combined with her black hair and eyes, called up the colors of a daisy. Reese was tempted to call her that and then, thinking it a poor joke, refrained.

"I need you to keep me honest," Reese said, moving toward her and extending the paper listing his expenses. "This is for tracking down Shep."

Jen accepted the paper and moved over to her desk and sat down. While she was reading the items, Reese moved to the straight-backed chair alongside the desk and slacked into it. He regarded Jen openly and lovingly and when she unaccountably looked up she surprised the naked look of longing in his eyes. It was as if, Reese thought, she was answering to a cry that had never been uttered before she returned her glance to the paper. Presently she said, "You're too honest, Reese. You must have called on a dozen ranches before you found Shep."

"I'm paid for that."

"Not when you're out of Sutton County."

Reese shook his head. "The hell with that. The only reason I made that list is because the commissioners will dog me until I do."

Jen smiled and tossed the paper on her desk. "All right. What you've listed are honest expenses. I'll swear to it if I have to."

Reese reached for the paper, folded it and stuck it in his shirt pocket as Jen asked idly, "What's new on the first floor?"

"Well, a man thinks we might have a rustling ring in Sutton County." He told her then of Reston's visit yesterday and of his opinion that his stolen cattle had been driven into the county.

When he finished, Jen said, "Unlikely, I should judge. Nobody new has moved into the county and if the natives were going to steal cattle, why haven't they stolen them before?"

"That's about what I told him," Reese said. Now he rose and they looked at each other almost hungrily.

"Still batching it?" Jen asked.

"No, Callie came home last night."

"Where did she spend her week?" Jen asked.

"With her aunt Amy Bashear."

"Heavens, I'd rather spend a week in jail."

"But you aren't a Hoad," Reese said wryly. When Jen said nothing, Reese said, "What was it you wanted in the top pigeon hole?"

"Fourth from the left."

Reese moved over to the rack and had to stretch the long length of him to reach the paper. He returned to the desk, gave it to Jen and said, "Why don't you lower that damn thing?"

"Dad put it up and he could reach everything."

"How's he doing?"

"The same." She grimaced slightly. "Everything's the same, isn't it?"

Reese nodded, turned and walked out.

He found himself making work for the rest of the day. His two weeks' freedom from Callie — his week and hers — had been surprisingly pleasant ones, reminiscent of the time before he was married. He had a faint feeling of shame when he recognized that he not only hadn't missed her but was glad that he didn't have to be with her. The sight of her when Ty brought her home last evening had brought back that feeling of quiet desperation so familiar to him. They had exchanged only moments of talk, mostly about Amy Bashear and the doings of her children and their children. The talk had bored him and Callie knew it and soon had gone to her room. Reese had read for a while in the kitchen, then gone to his room. He supposed this would be the pattern for all of his days.

Arriving at the Slash Seven now, he unsaddled, turned the horse out to pasture and stopped by the bunkhouse on his way. Ames Tolliver and Ryder were sitting on the bunkhouse steps and Reese halted and got the report from Ames of the day's work. The last rain, Ames reported, had been a godsend. They would not have to move to summer range for another ten days.

They chatted a moment and Reese turned and headed for the house. Then he halted abruptly and said to Ames, "Tell the boys to keep an eye out for any R-Cross branded beef, will you, Ames?"

"R-Cross? Whose brand is that?" Ames' thick-lensed spectacles emphasized the bewilderment in his eyes.

"A Texas brand. A trail herd was stampeded on the National last week. The owner thinks some of them might have drifted as far as here."

Ames nodded and Reese moved toward the house. There was no sense in telling Ames of Reston's suspicion of rustling, since the story would soon blow into a rumor that could not be stopped.

At the house he entered through the kitchen door and hung his hat on the nail inside. Everything was the same, he thought. Callie, in her drab dress, was at the stove, and when she turned to greet him, he saw the apathy in her eyes. He noticed now something that he had been too indifferent to notice last night. Callie's sallow complexion held a faint sunburn. He supposed that she and the Bashear girls had done some riding this past week. He went through the nightly ritual of washing and making a drink for Callie and himself. He put both drinks on the kitchen table and sat down. Presently, Callie moved over to her drink, took a sip and then asked indifferently, "What's happened in town, Reese? Amy's girls never go in, and you wouldn't even tell me if the town had burned down."

Her tartness of speech hadn't diminished since their quarrel, and Reese supposed that he had been thoroughly discussed by the Bashears, and that Callie had been the recipient of quite a bit of female sympathy. Well, what had happened in town while she had been away?

He said, "Tom Burbank's mare foaled an albino colt, ugly as sin. And a trail boss came yesterday and thought we might have rustlers in Sutton County. He got stampeded on the National. Jim Daley got a sprung back from being pitched off that bay of his." He paused. "I guess that does it."

When he looked up, Callie had her back to him at the stove, her glass in her hand.

"Rustlers in Sutton County," she repeated. "Do you believe that?"

"No. If I were you, I wouldn't repeat it. That's the way crazy rumors start and it wouldn't look good coming from the wife of the Sheriff."

Without turning Callie said in a voice that held a quaver of what Reese thought was anger, "Who would I tell it to? I never see anyone."

"Your family for one."

Now Callie turned and Reese saw that the

color had fled from her face. "Then you shouldn't have told me," she said angrily.

"You asked what had happened and I told you. Now keep it quiet." There was an edge of anger in his own voice but he didn't realize it was there until after he'd spoken.

"Yes, master," Callie said sardonically.

Reese thought wryly then that it had taken them less than ten minutes to get back to the edgy, suspicious and defensive relationship of two weeks ago. And why hadn't she said anything about the Hoad Land & Cattle Company? He sipped at his drink and suddenly found that he didn't want it. What in God's name was the use of their living together when each day they destroyed a little more of each other? But what galled him and shamed him was the realization that he was as much to blame as Callie.

The next morning Callie waited until Reese left for work and then swiftly she changed from her dull dress into a divided skirt, one of Reese's old shirts and riding boots. At the corral Sam obligingly got her horse from the horse pasture and saddled up for her. Afterwards she headed south for her father's spread. It was a sunny morning holding little wind. Every stock tank and every depression still held water from last week's torrential rain.

The sleepless night, however, had dulled her sensibilities and she was blind to the sleek cows and their fat calves she saw, even to the newly replenished graze.

To an impartial observer approaching it, Ty Hoad's Hatchet Ranch would have seemed a sorry affair that held an indefinable aura of failure. The buildings were in bad repair and the sod-roofed house and shadeless yard had a hard-scrabble look about them. The ranch with its poor range had changed hands three times in the last ten years. If a man owning it caught an easy winter and a wet spring, he could make out, but normally he fought a hard winter and a dry spring and summer. Afterwards he started looking for a buyer.

The buildings were two single-storey log houses connected by a dog run. They were built of huge cottonwood logs by the original builder who sacrificed the pleasure of shade and greenery to the necessity for shelter. The old stumps still pocked the area between the house and the sagging, jerrybuilt outbuildings of the corrals. No successor, including Ty, had bothered to plant anything.

Callie dismounted, loosened the cinch of her saddle and, turning her horse into the corral, strode swiftly among the stumps and past the bunkhouse where Ty's two Mexican cowhands bedded down. She even passed the open door to Ty's and Buddy's shack, heading for the spot where she knew she would find her father.

Turning the corner, she saw her father seated on the dirty shuck mattress of the rusted iron bedframe. Here, on the north side of the house, there was always shade. Ty spent a good part of his days there and slept there at night, preferring it to the airless and almost furnitureless cabin.

Ty, dressed in his ill-fitting range clothes, did not look up from mending a bridle as Callie came around the corner, crossed before him and sat down on the bed.

"I saw you coming," Ty said.

"Pa, we might be in trouble," Callie said without preliminaries. She spoke so quickly that Ty, after spitting through his already stained moustache, looked up. "Where's Buddy?" Callie said then.

"Him and Orv left early for town yesterday. Ain't seen him since. What trouble?"

Callie told him then of her conversation with Reese last night. They had both been feisty, she said, after Callie demanded to know what had gone on in her absence. He had told her of the trail boss's visit to him, during which he gave Reese his opinion that there were rustlers in Sutton County. Reese, Callie said, didn't think so but he had abjured her to keep silent lest foolish talk get around.

"Reese going to do anything about it?"

"I couldn't ask him any more for fear of seeming too curious, but I don't think so."

Ty looked off across at the low clay hills, whose now dried out tops trailed faint banners of dust pushed by a persistent though gentle wind.

"If he's not curious, then why you worried, Callie?"

"I don't rightly know, Pa. I'm just uneasy. Shouldn't we move those steers?"

"In a week we will."

"Shouldn't we warn the boys?" Callie persisted.

Ty snorted and looked pityingly at her. "Orv and his boys and Buddy, but nobody else. Reese was right. Enough people hear stock's been rustled, they'll start wondering where it's hid. Then Reese will start looking, for damn sure."

Callie stood up. "Pa, let's find Uncle Orv and see what he says."

"Why, he'll say the same as me," Ty said testily. "You fool women panic too easy."

"All right," Callie said coldly. "If those cattle are found with my brand on them, who's in trouble?" When her father looked at her in astonishment at her tone of voice, she held his glance without faltering.

"You trying to act like a president of a cattle company?"

"Yes," Callie said flatly. "You and Uncle Orv set me up there and you better protect me."

Her father sighed and put the bridle down. "All right, Callie. We'll go."

Together they walked to the corral where Ty cinched up Callie's saddle and saddled his own mount. Watching him Callie knew that she had offended him, but every word she said had been true. If the cattle were discovered, their brands unhealed, it would be she who would be questioned after Reese looked up the brand registration in the company incorporation.

Maybe he wouldn't have to look up either, for although he had never asked her about the Hoad Land & Cattle Company, he might know of its existence. He could be sly, Callie thought resentfully. Then she wondered if he was being sly when he said he didn't think there was any rustling in Sutton County. Was he baiting a trap and did he know more than he pretended? These were questions Uncle Orv could answer better than her father, for he was a shrewder man and, Callie admitted to herself now, more of a man than her father.

As they approached Orville Hoad's sagging gate, Callie could see Min Hoad seated in one of the veranda chairs and at this distance Callie guessed by her actions that the big, raw-boned, halfbreed Ute woman was shelling peas or stripping beans. Ty opened the sagging wire gate and passed Callie through, then, not bothering to mount, led his horse alongside Callie's the fifty yards up to the veranda.

Their greetings were pleasant enough, although Min, while counted a Hoad, was not really one of them. She was a square-faced, pleasantly homely woman who had done an adequate job of raising their children until Orville took them over and shaped them into Hoads. Quiet to taciturnity and shy, she was taken into the family's councils but her opinions were never sought.

Callie liked her and at any other time would have enjoyed chatting with her, but immediately upon dismounting now she said, "Min, is Uncle Orv here?"

"Him and Buddy are asleep in the bunkhouse. They got in a couple of hours ago."

Callie turned to her father. "Pa, go wake Uncle Orv or I will."

"If he's sleeping this time of day, he needs to," Ty protested.

"Will you do it or will I?" Callie challenged.

Grumbling under his breath, Ty headed toward the barn lot and bunkhouse close to a thick cluster of giant cottonwoods while Callie mounted the step to the veranda and took one of the rocking chairs. What did it take to make her father see the danger they were in, she wondered half in anger. Maybe Orville could impress him. Or was it as her father said, she was a panicky woman? Min, who had never started a conversation in anyone's memory, was not starting one now and Callie was thankful.

When Ty and Orville appeared, they came through the house. Orville stepped through the doorway, a half-full pitcher of moonshine dangling from his hand. His pale hair was awry and he was shirtless. He had hauled on a pair of pants held up by suspenders over his long underwear and since he didn't speak to Callie or look at her as he crossed before her to a chair, she guessed that he was in a bad mood. Orville slacked into the chair with a groan he did not try to suppress. Then, before he spoke, he lifted the pitcher and drank not from its spout but from its rim. While he was drinking Ty came over and took the chair beside him.

When Orville caught his breath, he looked harshly at Callie. "My God, girl, you aim to kill me?"

"No, Uncle Orv, but I didn't think this could wait."

"Ty's already told me what you come for. Is that all Reese told you? That this trail boss figured there was rustlers in Sutton County?"

Callie nodded. "I couldn't ask him more, could I? He'd think it was funny if I did. I never ask about the sheriffing business, so why should I now?" Only when she finished speaking did Callie realize how shrill her voice had been.

"He never said anything about what made this R-Cross rider suspicious?"

"Pa told you what Reese said. I asked him if he thought there were rustlers in Sutton County and he said no. Then he told me to keep my mouth shut about this. He didn't want rumors starting up."

"Now why wouldn't he?" Orv asked softly.

"That's one of the things I wanted to ask you."

"You figure this R-Cross rider told him things he wants to check out on the quiet before a lot of talk messes it up?"

"Do you?" Callie countered.

Orville leaned back in his chair and scratched under his armpit. "The only other reason he'd tell you to keep quiet is because he don't want to spend a lot of time looking for proof of rustling. I don't reckon that'd be the reason because Reese ain't a lazy man."

"So you think he might be investigating on the quiet?" Callie asked.

"If I knew what that trail boss told him,

I could answer you. I just don't know, Callie."

"Shouldn't we move the cattle, Uncle Orv?"

"When the brands are healed," Orville said. Now he took another drink of whisky and passed the pitcher to Ty, who shook his head in refusal. Orville cradled the pitcher in his lap between his big hands and continued. "I sent June and Emmett up to Big John this morning." Now he glanced at his wife. "Them boys have enough Injun in them to find out if there's any strangers hanging around that Copper Canyon country."

"Is that all we can do — just wait?"

"There's nothing else to do, unless you can get it out of Reese without him knowing it what this R-Cross rider told him."

Ty spoke up now. "Don't try it, Callie. Reese is smart. If he suspicioned us, we got trouble."

Orville swivelled his head to look at him. "If he don't find the cows, Ty, we ain't in real bad trouble."

"How so?"

Orville looked at Callie now. "That R-Cross rider ain't going to complain any more. He just won't be around again."

"You can be sure of that?" Callie asked.

"Buddy and me made sure," Orville said.

For a moment Callie didn't understand. "You mean you scared him off?"

"Well, you could call it that," Orville said judiciously. "He won't be a witness to anything. He's at the bottom of a mine shaft."

"You're holding him?" Callie asked.

Orville shook his head. "Buddy and me ain't. The mine shaft is."

Only then did Callie begin to comprehend. "He's dead."

Quietly then Orville told of seeing the R-Cross branded bay in front of the Best Bet and of talking with Will Reston about R-Cross strays he'd seen. On the road to find them he told of trying to learn what Reston had told Reese and when Reston told him that he was going back to the Little Muddy to get an R-Cross rider who could identify one of the rustlers, Orville knew he had to act. He simply shot Reston, disposed of the body and he and Buddy had ridden over to the Little Muddy looking for the injured man's camp. It wasn't there and had never existed. Reston had lied and had died for his lie. What he did not tell Callie was that he and Buddy couldn't find Reston's horse.

Callie heard him out with a strange calm and was not surprised at her own lack of revulsion or feeling of guilt. After all, had she ever really believed her Uncle Orville innocent of Flowers' death, even though she pretended to Reese she had believed so? And why had she agreed to head the Hoad Land & Cattle Company if she had not believed that her Uncle Orville was strong, a man of decision even if that decision meant violence? This, she had been taught, was the way a strong man should live, taking what he could, fighting for it and doing what was necessary to attain it and hold it. How else could any of the Hoads lift themselves out of this hard-scrabble existence unless they fought? The death of Will Reston was only part of that fight. If it was hard and cruel, that was all right too. Wasn't she on the receiving end of Reese's hardness and cruelty? In this last year she had come to believe that this was the way life was — unfair, mean and unrelenting. No, either it seized you by the throat or you seized it.

Now she felt herself relax for the first time since Reese had told her of the trail boss's visit. Uncle Orville was right. His boys could guard the camp, the trail boss was out of the way. If the man had told Reese that one of his riders could identify one of the rustlers, then Reese would wait for him in vain. If he hadn't told him that, then perhaps it was true that Reese really believed that there was no gang of rustlers in Sutton County.

Now Callie looked at her father to see how he had received the news of Reston's disposal. His round face held a lingering look of surprise and mild shock as if this news was something he hadn't bargained for. It held something else too that filled Callie with quiet elation: it was a look of resignation. Once more, it seemed to say, the Hoads had closed ranks.

Ty said then, "Seems like it's up to Reese to make the first move."

"If he makes any at all," Orville replied with quiet confidence.

The Bale House stood catty-corner from the brick Bank, a frame, two-storey building that had a veranda running its length on Main Street, joined with the veranda that ran its depth along Grant Street. There must have been thirty chairs on the big, L-shaped, railed veranda. During the day, when the sun touched the Main Street section, or horse and wagon traffic stirred up too much dust, a man simply left his chair on the Main Street side and went around the corner to a chair on the Grant Street side. At night, of course, Main Street side was the favorite because it had two entrances into the hotel and one of them was the doorway into the quiet saloon. Rather than the court-house or the Best Bet or Macey's, the Bale House veranda was the place to loaf, to trade or to conduct formal business. In a way it took the place of the shaded plazas in the Spanish towns further south, except that the plazas permitted women to mingle and gossip there while no woman, unless accompanied by a man, ever sat on the Bale House veranda.

Today there was a woman sitting on the Grant Street veranda after the noonday meal and she was Jen Truro. She was accompanied by the required male, who was Reese Branham. Their presence together for dinner in the Bale House dining room had long ceased to attract attention, for it was well known by everyone that the Sheriff must work under the direction of the District Attorney or his Deputy.

Reese tossed his hat on to one of the empty barrel chairs, then sat down next to Jen. He wiped a match alight on the veranda floor boards and lit a crooked black after-dinner Cheroot.

On the days when Jen was particularly busy, she fixed a cold lunch for Sebastian, and this was one of those days. A Sheriff's Sale of a failed boarding-house and its contents had to be appraised for the court, and Jen and Reese had spent the morning on this chore and would spend the afternoon. It was a hot day and breathless here in town. Perspiration stained the back and sides of Reese's starless cotton shirt, but Jen looked wonderfully cool in a primrose-colored cotton dress with green trim.

"Let's take our time getting back to that oven," Reese said, then added resignedly, "Lord, the things a sheriff is supposed to do. Price sheets, and how do you price sheets? Are they well worn, little worn, or new?"

"How do you price a shuck mattress?" Jen countered.

They were watching the lazy noon wagon and horse traffic, when Reese saw a rider leading a saddled horse scan the Bale House veranda and then cut across the street to the tie-rail in front of it. He was Con Fraley, who with his childless wife ran a twenty-cow outfit over by the brakes that barely fed them. Con was a little man in shabby range clothes, who was born to failure and seemed to know it and not care. He dismounted now, wrapped the reins of his horse over the tie-rail, then tied the other horse by its lead rope alongside his own. He swung under the tie-rail now and mounted the steps and headed for Reese.

As he approached he wrenched off his battered hat, revealing a pale, bald skull. Halting before Reese, he said, "Figured to find you here, Sheriff."

"What's on your mind, Con?" Reese asked.

Con turned to the two horses that he had just haltered and pointed with a thrust of his chin. "Found that gelding yesterday or I reckon he found me. He was with my horses

110

down at the seep below the house. He was saddled just like he is now except the reins were trailing and out. It's a brand I don't know, so I can't return him."

"What brand?"

"R-Cross, I read it."

Reese swivelled his glance to Jen and saw her watching him. Now he rose and went down the steps, took the break in the tie-rail and walked over to the two horses. Con trailed him in silence.

Reese halted and looked over the bay. There was a cut along his right wither that obviously had been doctored recently. He went over to examine the three-inch raw furrow in the flesh. It was not ragged enough to have come from wire or brush, and Reese guessed immediately that a bullet had made it. Furthermore, the bullet had travelled from back to front for the frayed flesh around its exit pointed towards the bay's head.

"He had that cut when he come up to our place. Flies been after it, so I cleaned it up."

Reese noted the short hoof-cut reins tied over the bay's neck. The saddle, old and worn, was free of stain and Reese realized suddenly that he was looking for blood stains that weren't there. He decided now that if Con hadn't guessed the cut was a bullet wound, he wasn't going to tell him.

He only said, "That's a Texas brand, Con. He's from a trail herd that's long gone."

Con looked at him admiringly now. "How d'you know that?"

Reese looked down at him and smiled. "You pick up a lot of stray information in this office, Con." He looked at the brand again and said, "I'm obliged to you for bringing him in. Drop him off at Miller's, will you, Con, and tell them he's a County charge."

Con nodded. "He looks poorly."

"A few oats will fix that," Reese said and turned back to the veranda. He stood beside his chair and watched Con ride off towards the feed stable, then he sat down.

"That man you said complained to you about being rustled, wasn't his brand R-Cross?" Jen asked.

Reese looked at her now. "Yes."

"Is that his horse?"

Reese tossed his half-smoked stub out into the street and said, "That's what I'm going to find out, Jen. You're on your own this afternoon. Mind?"

"No. Your heart isn't in it anyway."

They fell silent then and Reese gazed moodily at the street. He was remembering the day Reston came in. Unlike most of the riders who had business in the Sheriff's office, Reston hadn't tied his horse out of the sun under the

112

horse shed. He might have tied it at the front tie-rail before the court-house entrance which would be a natural thing to do if a man didn't know the location of the Sheriff's office in the court-house. Somebody there was bound to have seen the horse and remarked it, since the brand would be a strange one to anyone in Bale. Jen hadn't seen the bullet wound and he decided not to tell her about it either.

Now Reese picked up his hat, rose and said, "I'll stop by your house after I close up, Jen."

Jen rose too. "I'll have everything listed, Reese, when you come by."

They parted and Reese headed directly for the court-house. Somebody in the court offices on the first and second floors fronting the street must have seen Reston's horse at the tie-rail. As he tramped through the hot noon, he reckoned the day and the hour when Reston had visited him. The court-house bunch had just returned from dinner now. They were, Reese had learned, a loyal group, made so by politics, and also a gossipy one. Still, in the next half hour, Reese could find no one who remembered seeing the R-Cross bay on the morning of the date he mentioned. The county clerk, Abe Frohm, remembered a tall man in chaps enquiring for the Sheriff's office, but he hadn't bothered to look out and identify his horse and brand.

Back in his office Reese found Jim Daley at the desk and he slacked into the chair facing him. He told of Con Fraley's arrival at the Bale House with what could be Will Reston's horse, and he finished by saying quietly, "He's got a cut on his wither that looks like it came from a bullet."

Daley's square face, tight with the effort to hide the pain of his strained back, looked even grimmer at this news. "Did the bullet cut line up with the saddle?"

"If a man had been riding him, the bullet would have hit him in the right thigh before it went through his leg to cut the bay. But there was no blood on the saddle or stirrup, Jim."

Daley frowned. "He could have been drove out of the saddle."

"Not when you see the saddle. These trail hands like a big swell, and this had it. It would have anchored him like it was meant to."

Daley nodded thoughtfully.

Reese went on, "Somebody in town had to see that horse the day Reston was here. Nobody in the court-house did, but somebody had to." Now he pushed himself erect. "Come on down to the feed stable with me, Jim, and get a look at the bay so you can describe him. Then you start at the Bale House and I'll start at the other end of Grant Street. Ask in every

114

store if anyone remembers seeing Reston on that horse."

"A strange brand is always picked up in a town this size," Daley said. Now he wrenched himself out of his chair, grimacing in pain. Picking up his hat, he said, "Now describe me Reston."

On their way to the livery, Reese gave a description to Jim of Reston and what he was wearing. At the livery itself, Reese hunted up the saddle and put it on the bay that was in the feed corral with a half dozen other horses. Daley agreed with him that the bullet would have caught the rider in the thigh. They carefully searched the stirrup leathers for any sign of blood stains and found none. Afterwards they parted, but only after Reese quizzed Miller's hostlers. It seemed reasonable that Reston would have put up his horse for graining while he went about his business, but that hadn't happened. Then, store to store, one side of the street to the other, Reese worked his way down the street as far as the blacksmith's shop where he found Daley talking with Art Michaels and his helper. Reese walked in on the tail-end of the conversation, the gist of which was no, neither of them had seen or handled the bay branded R-Cross.

Outside they halted and Reese said, "I didn't turn up a thing. How about you?"

"Nothing — except, maybe, a little some-thing."

Reese scowled. "Like what?"

"Well, Perry Owens was back of the bar at the Best Bet that morning. He remembered Reston from the description, said he loafed around for a half hour and killed a couple of beers. He didn't talk to anybody and never opened his mouth except to ask for another beer."

"Well, what's the something, Jim?" Reese asked impatiently.

Jim shook his head. "I don't know. I just got the feeling, Reese, that Perry's telling the truth, but not all of it."

"Why do you?"

"Well, he remembered Reston real quick. He looked at me square with them bloodshot eyes of his while he talked about Reston, but when I asked him about the horse, he wouldn't look at me. He said he watched Reston leave and thought he rode a grey, but he couldn't be sure." Daley paused and shook his head. "If he admits seeing Reston go out and mount up, he'd sure as hell remember the color of his horse. He'd be sure it was a grey, wouldn't he? He wouldn't guess it was a grey."

Reese nodded. "Did he know why you were asking?"

"He pretended he didn't, but likely he did,"

Jim said grimly. "I reckon the minute I opened my mouth in the Bale House bar the news started to spread. It took me a half hour to reach the Best Bet, so he'd of heard."

Reese considered this a moment, wondering why Perry Owens wouldn't want to link Reston with his horse. Why would he lie or evade or pretend he couldn't positively link them? Now Reese said, "Let's go see Perry again."

Together they tramped up the boardwalk to the Best Bet and went inside. It was a slack hour and the only customers were a foursome of store clerks playing hearts at a back table. Perry Owens, with nothing better to do and no customers to attend to, was boredly watching the game. When Reese and Jim walked up to the bar, he left the game, came around the end of the bar and up to them. The apron that hung from his bony hips was already dirty and beer-slopped from the morning's trade, and the yellow-toothed smile he gave them as he halted before them was strained.

"Perry, give that apron to your swamper and come up the street with us," Reese said.

Perry's bloodshot eyes widened. "Where to?"

"You'll see. Maybe jail."

"Now wait a minute —" Perry began.

"Come along," Reese said curtly.

Perry hesitated, then turned back down the

117

bar, unknotting his apron as he walked. He paused in the door of the back room, called something to his swamper, put his apron on the bar and came up to join Reese and Jim. Once on the boardwalk and turned down the street, Perry, seeing the direction they were heading, said, "What's this, Reese?"

"I want to see if you're color-blind, Perry. If you are, I'm allowed to hold you for forty-eight hours, then I'll have to let you loose. But I'll be back to see if you're still color-blind, and if you still are, I'll hold you another forty-eight hours."

"I don't know what you're talking about," Perry said morosely.

"I think you do," Reese answered.

They turned in at the feed stable, walked its runway and halted at the horse corral. Reston's bay stood by himself, shunned as a stranger by the dozen livery horses that were old friends.

Reese pointed to him and said, "What color would you call that lone horse, Perry?"

"Why, bay. What else could he be?"

"Go face him to us, Jim, will you?"

Daley stepped through the gate, moved over to the bay and shouldered him in the neck until he faced Perry and Reese.

"That's the angle you'd have seen him from. Now have you seen him before?"

"My God, how can I remember?" Perry said irritably. "I probably look at a thousand bay horses a year."

"I think you remember him," Reese said quietly. "You changed his color to grey, but you weren't positive enough about it, Perry. You told Jim you *guessed* Reston rode a grey, but you know damn well he didn't."

Perry shrugged. "Well, if somebody else identified him as that rider's horse, then I guess I made a mistake."

"Don't guess any more, Perry," Reese said gently. "You guessed wrong once already." He paused. "Is that the horse Reston rode out on?"

"I don't know," Perry wailed. "Why? How am I to know what color horse every customer rides?"

"You said he was grey," Reese said and his voice held a quality of granite. "That means you looked at his horse. If you hadn't, all you had to do was say you never saw his horse, but you said you saw it and you said it was grey. You're lying, Perry. Why?"

By this time, Jim had come up to the corral posts and was listening. Perry looked from Reese to Jim and back again to Reese, and now his face was flushed with both shame and anger.

"All right, goddam it!" he burst out. "I'll

119

tell you. Yes, that's his horse. The reason I lied was because I seen Orville and Buddy Hoad talking with him, standing there by his horse. I figured that some trouble's come up about this horse and that rider. I don't want to tie no Hoad into it, so I lied."

"Why don't you want to tie a Hoad into it?" Reese asked.

"You got to ask me that?" Perry said angrily. "Hell, you get a Hoad mad at you, any one of his damn family would kill you. Look at Flowers. You think I want that?" Then he added bitterly, "You're a Hoad yourself by marriage. I want no part of the whole pack of you, even if you're Sheriff."

Reese looked at Daley now, and Jim avoided his eyes. What was it Jim had said? 'The Hoads ain't easy to like.'

"Why'd you say there was some trouble about Reston and his horse?"

"If there ain't any, you wouldn't be asking me to tie 'em together, would you?"

"No," Reese agreed. "Now tell me everything about Reston that happened that morning."

"I told you," Perry said shortly, impatiently. "Orville and Buddy come into the bar and asked whose bay that was. I said I didn't know — just some puncher come in, bought a beer and left. They went outside and waited and pretty soon this man come along and mounted up. Then Buddy and Orville talked with him a few minutes. Afterwards they left and like I said, he come in and had two beers. Then he rode off."

"All right, Perry, back to your booze. And thanks."

Even Perry's back looked righteously indignant as he headed back through the runway.

Reese and Jim looked at each other, and the older man's face held a faint embarrassment.

"What d'you think of it?" Reese asked him.

Jim shook his head. "Not much. Orville Hoad's got a right to speak to a stranger, just like you and me do. Because Perry's scared of the Hoads don't change that, does it?"

"No," Reese agreed. "Still, why did Orville and Buddy ask Perry about Reston and then wait for him?"

"Same answer, Reese. They were curious about the brand."

"Too curious?" Reese asked quietly.

Jim sighed. "I don't know how you judge that."

Now they left the corral and headed back toward the court-house.

It was Daley then who spoke first. "You think something's happened to Reston, Reese?"

"If he doesn't show up pretty soon, I'll think so."

"If his horse throwed him, he could have caught another or bought another from one of those spreads out by the brakes. Maybe he figured the hell with it and rode off to catch up with his herd."

"If you'd met Reston you wouldn't think that," Reese said dryly.

They parted at the court-house; Daley went inside, and Reese went back to the horse shed and saddled his grey. There was something ominous here, but he couldn't pin it down. Jim had been right when he said that Orville, and by implication Buddy too, had a perfect right to strike up an acquaintance with a stranger. Any stranger passing through Bale could bring news of the outside other world into their isolated one, and he was welcome for his gossip.

He mounted and headed up the back street toward the boarding-house where Jen was working, yet his uneasiness never ceased nagging at him. Why did it have to be Orville and Buddy who were seen talking with Reston? Why did they inquire about the owner of the R-Cross branded horse, and why were they willing to wait until he returned to his horse? That was more than idle curiosity, Reese judged.

He found the boarding-house locked, which meant that Jen had finished, and now he felt a strange relief. He would send Jim Daley to fetch the list for him, for he had other things in mind for the remainder of the afternoon. Back at the court-house he stopped only long enough to ask Jim to pick up the appraisal from Jen and then headed out of town, riding south for an hour in the blazing sun. At Orville Hoad's place he learned from Minnie that Orville and the three boys were out. She thought, but wasn't sure, that they were on a scout for some range in the Wheelers, she told him. Reese left word with her for Orville to drop in the court-house as soon as he could. Closing the sagging wire gate, Reese mounted again, already knowing what he was going to do.

3

He made directly for Ty Hoad's Hatchet Ranch. This, he reflected, was a mean country and the heat made it meaner. The whole range had lost the green of the last rain, and now its tan monotony shivered in the heat. Grazing cattle in the distance seemed to be moving up and down through the heat waves. Even Ty Hoad's barren Hatchet Ranch danced in the distance as he approached it.

Ty's two Mexican hands were at long last doing something about the sagging corral, he noted. As he rode past them he saluted lazily and they returned his greeting with an even lazier wave. He found some shade for his horse on the far side of the shack and left him there. When he rounded the corner of the house he found Buddy standing in the unshaded doorway. His pale hair was rumpled, his eyes puffy. Reese guessed that his coming had roused Buddy from a nap.

"You and Pa are both crazy to be out in this heat," Buddy greeted him. "He's headed for your place, and you're here. Didn't you meet him?" He stepped aside and Reese entered the mean single room. It was airless and stank of unwashed clothes and fried food. Buddy moved past him, heading for the cot and leaving the lone chair for Reese.

"No, I came from Orville's," Reese said.

Buddy veered over to a wall shelf and lifted down a crockery jug and Reese knew he was about to receive the invariable Hoad welcome, which consisted of a gagging drink of moonshine.

"Have a drink and set," Buddy said, as he lifted the jug down. "Pa'll be home before dark."

Reese slacked into the single straight-backed chair, saying mildly, "It's you I want to see, Buddy."

Buddy nodded, came over and extended the jug. Reese shook his head and said, "It's too hot for it, Buddy."

Now Buddy moved to the cot with his jug and sat down and tilted up a drink from it. Watching him, Reese felt a quiet, strong dislike for him, and he wondered guiltily if it was because, except for his size, Buddy was so like Callie in his actions and appearance.

When Buddy caught his breath, he observed, "It must be important as hell, whatever it is you come for, Reese."

"Not likely. Just information." Reese tilted his chair back against the wall and fumbled for the pipe and cut plug in his shirt pocket.

As he talked now he drew out his knife and cut off a bit of the plug and shredded it in his palms before loading it into his pipe.

"Buddy, you remember Tuesday of last week when you and Orville were in town?"

"Was it Tuesday? I lose track," Buddy said easily.

"Remember talking to a man in front of the Best Bet, a stranger?"

"Riding an R-Cross branded bay?"

Reese stifled his surprise at Buddy's candid answer. "He's the one," he said.

"Nice fellow," Buddy observed.

"How d'you and Orville happen to talk to him?"

"Why, hell, I don't know," Buddy said carelessly. Then he said, "Yes, I do. Uncle Orv spotted the brand and remembered where it come from."

"Where was that?"

"I think Uncle Orv said Big Spring — no, Big Island — Texas."

"How did Orv know that brand?"

Now Buddy leaned forward on the cot, placing his elbows on his knees. He looked at the floor, frowning and it was the first time his glance had left Reese's. Was it evasiveness? Reese wondered.

"Let's see," Buddy said thoughtfully. "Aunt Amy Bashear's boys make a trip down there a couple of times a year with two or three big wagons. They load 'em with ground sheets and tents and raw canvas. They'll hit these back country cow camps and trade for cows. Uncle Orv went with 'em once, and they traveled that Big Island country. Uncle Orv remembered the R-Cross brand, and he waited to find out from this pilgrim what the news was from down there."

When Buddy looked up now Reese was lighting his pipe but watching him over the burning match.

"You ride all the way out here to ask me that?" Buddy asked curiously.

"Looks like it."

"Why?" Buddy asked.

"His horse wandered in Con Fraley's place and Con brought him in. He'd been creased by a bullet."

Again Buddy's glance slid away, but he made a good attempt at framing a look of puzzlement. Had his face paled a little, Reese wondered. The whisky should have flushed it.

"Well, well," Buddy said idly. "What d'you make of that?"

"Nothing much — yet," Reese said. Then he added, "Did he tell you why he was in Bale?"

Buddy frowned and took a long time answering, as if he were trying to remember. "Said his trail herd got stampeded by that last storm, said he was looking for strays."

That sounded reasonable, Reese thought and asked, "What else did he talk about?"

"The Big Island country mostly. Families that Uncle Orv knew. Didn't mean nothing to me and I didn't really listen."

Reese observed now that Buddy was sweating. His upper lip was silver with perspiration. Still, it was an inferno in this room, and even though he hadn't had a drink of whisky, Reese felt drenched. "Anything else?" he asked.

"Cattle and horse prices, grass, just what any cowman would talk about."

Reese's pipe had gone out. He started to reach for a match to relight it and then changed his mind. All he really wanted was to get out of this oven, but he had one more question to ask. "Did he say he'd talked to me?"

Buddy shook his head in negation. (Was it too quickly?) "Not that I recollect."

With his shoulder Reese pushed his chair away from the wall and in the same motion rose. "Got anything besides whisky to drink, Buddy?" he asked, and then, thinking how superior he sounded, he added, "I'd like a crack at that jug, then a long drink of water."

Buddy grinned, put a finger in the jug handle and rose, moved over and extended the jug to his brother-in-law. Reese accepted it, took a small drink, put his tongue in the jug mouth and swallowed two more times. After he lowered the jug, he put back the corn cob stob and passed the jug back to Buddy. Then he moved over to the table which held the water pail and drank deeply of the tepid water from the tin dipper. Buddy trailed him to the door and halted there.

"If Pa's with Callie when you get there, tell him to bring some of Callie's bread back with him, Reese."

"I'll do that, Buddy," Reese said.

He got his horse, led him over to the scummed water tank by the corral where the two Mexican hands were working, called out, *"Como le va?"* Both men answered, *"Bien, Jertife."*

When his horse had drunk enough, Reese mounted and rode out. The sun had heeled far over by now and Reese rode into it, squinting against its full glare. What had Buddy really told him that mattered? Not much, he conceded sourly to himself. Buddy's and Orville's reasons for talking with Reston were reasonable, as was Buddy's account of what had been said. The only thing he hadn't asked Buddy to explain was how the Bashears had come up with a couple of wagon-loads of tents, ground sheets and canvas, but then he knew the answer to that without asking. The Bashears traded moonshine to the supply sergeant down at Fort Tipton in exchange for any supplies the sergeant could steal and cover up for. This all happened outside of Sutton County and was no concern of his.

Now he tried to sum up his observations on the way Buddy acted during their conversation. He could find nothing to flesh out a suspicion. Buddy's reaction to the news of the discovery of Reston's horse was a natural one — moderate surprise, then puzzlement, but not concern. *Why should he show concern?* Reese thought. If what had passed between Orville, Buddy and Reston was as inconsequential as Buddy made out, why should he show concern? Still, Reese had a deep distrust of the Hoads, any Hoad, and he had learned the hard way that they were all consummate actors in their backwoods way.

Why, after Orville Hoad's acquittal and the bitter resentment of all the Hoads toward his part in the trial, was Buddy so friendly this afternoon? A surliness, a to-hell-with-you attitude would have been more in character for Buddy. This afternoon he'd been reasonable when Reese least expected him to be.

This damn family, he thought grimly. They knew he was their enemy and forgiveness was not in their character. Yet Minnie and Buddy had been civil enough, even friendly and that, too, Reese thought, was passing strange.

He didn't meet Ty Hoad on his way back home. At the Slash Seven he unsaddled and turned out his horse, noting that neither Ty's horse nor the crews' best mounts were here.

A familiar feeling of depression came over him then as he headed toward the house. Would it be tonight that Callie would mention the Hoad Land & Cattle Company? Each night since she had returned from the Bashears he had waited for her to say something.

As he approached the house, Reese saw Callie on her knees before a flower bed that flanked the front door. She looked up and Reese called, "Let's have a drink out here, Callie."

"All right." Her voice held an indifference that was unmistakable.

Reese went into the kitchen which the stove, holding their cooking supper, made unbearably hot. He hung his hat on the peg, quickly made their two whiskys and water and stepped outside with the drinks. Callie had abandoned her gardening and was now seated in the old rocker under the big cottonwoods. She was wearing a discarded shirt of his and a pair of his castaway pants, the legs rolled up almost to the knees. For some reason Reese was unable to understand, Callie, since her visit to the Bashears had tried to make herself as unattractive as possible. Her ordinary house dresses were drab enough, but they were preferable to his cast-off clothes. He handed her a drink and then seated himself on the semicircular bench at the base of the cottonwood. As he leaned back against the rough bark, he noticed her face held a faint suspicion and he wondered what had provoked it.

"You came in across the horse pasture," Callie said. "Were you at Pa's?"

When Reese nodded, Callie said, "Why?"

"I really wanted to see Orville but he was out, and I stopped by to see Buddy."

"What for?" Callie asked, so swiftly that Reese looked at her in mild surprise.

"You remember me telling you about the trail driver that had his herd stampeded?" he asked.

"The one I wasn't supposed to talk about?"

"That's the one. Con Fraley found his saddled horse and brought it in today. He'd been nicked by a bullet."

Now Callie raised her drink to her lips, and Reese noted that her hand was unsteady and guessed it was because she had been tugging at the weeds in the flower garden. She took a sip and then asked, "What do you make of that?"

"I don't know what to make of it."

Callie frowned. "Where's the connection between Uncle Orv, Buddy and this horse?"

"Orv and Buddy were seen talking to this man Reston in town."

"Well, what if they were?" Callie asked sharply.

"I just wondered why."

"Did Buddy tell you?"

Reese nodded and took a sip from his drink while Callie watched him with hard and searching eyes. Then he said, "Buddy said Orv recognized the brand of the horse Reston was riding. Orv had been down in Reston's country on a trading trip with the Bashears. He just wanted to ask after some folks he knew down that way."

"You sound like you didn't believe Buddy," Callie said flatly.

Reese frowned. "Do I? I didn't mean to."

"Well, you did," Callie snapped. "You always sound like you don't believe anything a Hoad says."

Reese felt a sudden, unreasoning anger, but he managed to keep it out of his voice as he said, "Come to think of it, I don't."

"How can you say that?" Callie demanded fiercely.

"Well, we both saw Orv on the witness stand and heard him lie under oath."

"That's a damn lie!" Callie said flatly.

"It isn't a lie," Reese said. "It may be a wrong opinion, but it isn't a lie."

"Why did you have to ask Uncle Orv and Buddy what they talked to Reston about? Why didn't you ask other people what they talked to him about?"

"Reston talked to me, asked the bartender for two beers and talked with Buddy and Orv. We're the only people he talked to."

"But what does it matter who talked to him? What business is it of yours anyway?"

"If a man disappears, we try and find out why," Reese said flatly. "That is, you do if you're Sheriff."

"You think he's disappeared," Callie said jeeringly. "What proof have you?"

"Just that his saddled horse walked in with a gunshot wound."

"Are you trying to lay that on Uncle Orv and Buddy?"

Reese said angrily, "Goddam it, woman, no!"

"Don't you swear at me!"

"I'm not swearing at you, I'm swearing in front of you," Reese said shortly. He drained his drink, got up and headed for the kitchen door to make himself another. What had turned Callie from an almost pathetically docile woman into a demanding shrew? The answer to that, he knew, was that he himself had. As he mixed another drink for himself, he thought that wasn't entirely true. Callie was getting obsessed with her belief that the Hoads were being persecuted. Perhaps that was natural since if she couldn't turn to him, she must turn to them. Yet she seemed totally blind to their faults, unable to see that her father was a shiftless fraud, her brother a lazy whore-chaser, her uncle a killer and her cousins illiterate clods, all of them living in a half-drunken state of irresponsibility.

He took his drink now and moved out again to the bench and sat down. Callie watched him, and when he was seated, she said shortly, "You might have asked me if I wanted another drink."

"If you want a second drink, it will be for the first time since we've been married," Reese said dryly. "Do you?"

"No. I just want to be asked."

Reese looked at her closely. "If you want to be asked, I'll ask you some things."

Callie looked both indignant and a little fearful. "What things?"

"You're president of the Hoad Land & Cattle Company," Reese said calmly. "What's it all about?"

Callie eyed him levelly and a flush came over her face, whether from embarrassment or anger Reese didn't know. "That's my business," she said coldly.

"I know. But what land, what cattle?"

"I guess us Hoads own a lot of land, don't we? Maybe it isn't the best, but if we can sell it for a profit, why shouldn't we?"

"Who's us Hoads?" Reese demanded.

"All of us!" Callie said angrily. "Pa and Uncle Orv, the Bashears, the Plunkets, the Maceys — you know who as well as I do."

"Where do the cattle come from?" Reese asked.

"We're going to buy them or trade for them, fatten them up and sell them. It's just like a big ranch operation with all us thrown in together."

Reese asked almost idly then, "Bought any cows yet?"

Callie hesitated and Reese caught the hesitation. Then she said, almost too quickly, "No, we've only started."

"Where you going to run these cows you'll buy?"

"I told you," Callie said irritably. "Between us we've got grass for a lot more cattle than we're running." Now she stood up and said shortly, "I've got to get supper." She turned and Reese watched her as she moved toward the house, a kind of nameless dread coming over him. Callie was lying and evading, intuition told him. Between them, all the Hoads couldn't raise the price of two dozen cows. No bank would loan them money on their generally worthless range, trifling equipment or their cull cattle. No one in his right mind would go on a Hoad note, and the fact that neither Callie nor any other Hoad had suggested that he go on their notes was evidence in itself that this wasn't a serious and open business operation.

Where then would they get their money to buy stock or get stock? *They'd steal it,* he thought bleakly. Had they stolen it already, starting their venture with R-Cross cattle?

Now Reese leaned his head back against the tree and closed his eyes, fighting a sickness that seemed to reach into his very being. *This can't be,* he told himself, but then he knew it very well could be. The Hoads were capable of it — capable too of playing on Callie's insane family loyalty to drag her into it. Her own hatred of him would have influenced her too.

What in God's name was he to do? he wondered.

He finished his drink and gently set the glass down on the bench. Looking at this coldly now he knew that he had no proof of his suspicions, nor was there any way to get proof without tipping them off that the lot of them were suspect. If they thought he was investigating them, the result was predictable. With twenty odd Hoads just waiting for the right opportunity, he could expect a gunfight against wild odds or even ambush. His marriage to a Hoad wouldn't save him for he, reluctantly accepted by them, would have turned against them. They would remember that he tried to hang Orville and was now trying to destroy them all. Well, he could face that when the time came, but that time wasn't now.

"Your supper's ready," Callie called from the kitchen door. Reese rose, empty glass in hand, and crossed the yard to the kitchen. Moving toward the table in the stifling room, he halted abruptly, then looked at Callie by the stove.

"There's only one place set. Aren't you eating?"

"No. I'm going to ride over to Pa's."

"To tell him what we've talked about?"

Callie shrugged. "What's there to tell? I just want to see him."

"You saw him this afternoon."

"How d'you know that?" Callie flared.

"Buddy told me he was here."

"He was and he went into town to talk with Martin Farmer about some papers I'll have to sign."

"Let him bring them over here." There was an anger in Reese's voice that he could not disguise.

"No, I'll go over there and sign them." Callie's voice was adamant if sweetly patient. "Then I'll cook up something for Buddy and Pa. They never eat unless I make them."

Reese knew she was lying about having to sign papers. Something said in their conversation had alarmed Callie and she wanted to alert her father and the others. He could forbid her to go but what would that accomplish? Minutes after he rode out tomorrow morning she would be headed for her father. Now he shrugged and said idly, "Suit yourself."

"That's just what I'm doing from now on," Callie said. She spoke quietly too.

She went out and Reese stood motionless, appalled at the events of this day and their implications.

Callie arrived at Hatchet just at dusk. A lamp was already lighted in the bunkhouse, but her father's house was dark. When she dismounted at the corral she saw another horse tied there and recognized it as her Uncle Orville's. That was good, she thought grimly. There were a few things to be settled tonight.

Buddy, her father and Uncle Orville were where she expected to find them, seated on the old bed back of the shack. As she rounded the corner their conversation stopped. Ty seemed too surprised to even greet her, but Orville said, "Why, Callie, girl," by way of greeting. Callie only nodded and moved over to the empty rocking chair. She didn't sit down, however, but moved in behind it and leaned on its back. She remembered enough of school to know that the teacher who stood always had the advantage over the pupil who sat. She was not aware of how she looked until Buddy said, "Something eatin' you, Sis?"

"You should talk," Callie said derisively, angrily. She looked from Buddy to Orville. "Uncle Orv, you never told me Reston's horse got loose that day."

"Well, you never asked, Callie. I reckon I just plumb forgot it."

Callie looked at Buddy now. "You hid it on purpose, didn't you, Buddy?"

Buddy smiled faintly. "I reckon. We couldn't catch him or shoot him and that's a fact. What good would it be to have you frettin' about it and hackin' at us for missin' him?"

"It would have saved me from hearing it from Reese and damn near fainting!" Callie said angrily.

"Now, now," Orville said soothingly.

"I don't care!" Callie raged on. "What if

I had fainted? I almost did. If I hadn't had a drink in my hand to swallow, I would have."

"Did Reese notice?" Ty asked.

"I don't know. We had a fight. He knows about the company."

"I figured he would. We even wanted him to. You know that," Orville said and then asked, "What did he say?"

Now Callie came around the chair and sank into it. "He asked me where we were going to get the land and the cattle." Now, her anger subsiding, she told of Reese's sceptical questioning. "I shut him off as quick as I could, but he'll be back at it," she finished.

"He's got us tied in with the R-Cross beef?" Buddy asked.

"You should know that better than I do. Did he mention it?"

"No, I did," Buddy said with pride in his voice. "I told him Reston was looking for strays from a stampede and that's how come he was in Bale."

"Buddy did good," Orville said quietly. "We got together on that story just in case Reese got nosy."

"By damn, why don't you tell me these things!" Callie asked hotly, angered afresh. "I've got to live with him! I've got to answer the questions! How can I when you won't tell me what to answer?"

"You ain't ever around when we think of them, Callie, and we don't none of us like to go to your place, except Ty. He's your Pa and I don't reckon Reese would throw him off like he would us."

"No, you make me come to you instead, like now! Reese knows I'm here and he doesn't like it any. I lied about some papers Pa had for me and he knew I lied."

"Hell, Sis, be sensible," Buddy said. "I couldn't cut over to tell you about the horse when Reese was headed for home too."

"Yeah. You come all the way over here to scold us for that?" Orville asked.

"Partly, but mostly something else." She paused to emphasize what she was about to say. "We've got to get that herd out of Copper Canyon, Uncle Orv."

"Oh, do we," Orville said softly.

It was getting too dark to see his face but Callie knew what it would reflect — mockery, defiance and contrariness. She was a little afraid of what that expression portended, and now she tried to control her anger. "Look, Uncle Orv, this isn't a foolish woman talking. I've lived with Reese, and I know how he thinks. Will you believe that?"

"Why, I have to."

"And here's what I think he'll do," Callie said. "Reese believed Buddy's story today about your talk with Reston, but if Reston doesn't show up in a couple of days, Reese is going to believe that Reston was right. There is rustling here. He's going to think that Reston maybe tangled with the rustlers because of his shot horse. Then he's going to start looking for the rustled cattle. If we leave them where they are, he'll find them, sure as my name's Callie Hoad."

"But your name ain't Callie Hoad," Buddy pointed out and laughed.

"As far as I'm concerned, it is. Everything I'm telling you is the God's truth."

They were all quiet, impressed by the conviction with which Callie had spoken. Finally Orville said, "Callie, it's too soon after that stampede to sell those cows. They're fresh branded."

"No," Callie said flatly. "It's been two weeks since they've been branded. By the time you get them across the mountains, it'll be three weeks or a month. You've had time to drive 'em up from North Texas to wherever you sell 'em." She paused. "You've got to remember something, Uncle Orv. Around here only Reese, Jim Daley, that bitch of a woman lawyer and us know there was a stampede on the National. Over the Wheelers they won't have heard of it."

Orville didn't answer immediately, and

Buddy and his father were silent, deferring to him. Finally he said, "I reckon you're right, Callie girl. We could have made that drive in a month like you say." He paused. "But, dang it, I hate running."

"You hate running more than you like money?" Callie asked tartly. "More than you hate jail?"

"There'll be no more jail for me," Orville said quietly, in a tone of voice that implied that this was not only a foolish question, but an unnecessary one.

Ty spoke up now. "Move the cattle, Orv — unless you want Reese to brace you."

"Oh, that'll come anyway," Orville said placidly.

"How'd you figure that, Uncle Orv?" Buddy asked.

"Why, he hit me. We'll meet."

Ty said quietly, "But it shouldn't be over this, Orv."

"No," Orville agreed. Now he swivelled his head to address Buddy. "You'd better start for Copper Canyon now, Buddy. Tomorrow you and the boys get the cattle moving. Push 'em hard to the County Line. That's the Divide. Once you're across, take your time. Send Big John down to Moffitt. I'll be there."

I won, Callie thought elatedly. *I'm going to keep on winning too.*

144

★ ★ ★

Next morning the Sheriff's Sale of the boarding-house and its contents was held on the court-house steps before a dozen of the town's loafers and only one serious bidder. Mrs. O'Rourke, a scrappy, handsome, healthy widow, bid in at the lowest price the commissioners had agreed to accept and there were no other bidders. It was over almost before it began. Reese escorted Mrs. O'Rourke to his office, made out a check for the sum bid, watched while Mary Coughlin O'Rourke laboriously printed out her name, gave her the key to the house and the inventory of contents, wished her good luck and afterwards sat down to wait for Jim Daley, whom he had left in conversation with one of the spectators.

After the events of yesterday he wondered what this day would bring, and he hoped fervently that it would bring Will Reston. If Reston's bay had wound up at Con Fraley's, it was reasonable to assume that he had come out of the bordering brakes. If Reston could walk, surely he would have made one of the ranches close to the brakes. Surely too his first move would be to come to this office or send word for the Sheriff to come to him. If he was hurt and unable to walk, then he would surely die. It would take fifty men fifty days to search thoroughly the wild waterless can-

145

yons and caves and rimrock of that country. The County had no funds to pay for this broad search, and he had no right to ask for volunteers to give up the rest of the summer on the hunt for a man whom death perhaps had already silenced and whom the carrion birds would long since have disposed of. A live Reston, or word of him, must come to him, hopefully today, certainly by tomorrow. If he didn't come, then what? He didn't know.

Jim Daley, who had come straight from home to the court-house steps, had had no chance to speak with Reese, and now when he came in, he went directly to the chair beside the desk and eased into it.

"How's the back this morning, Jim?"

"You don't hear me whistling, do you?" Jim said wryly. Abruptly then he came to the point. "You find Orv or Buddy?"

"Buddy," Reese said. He told Jim of their reason for accosting Reston.

When he'd finished, Daley said, "Sounds harmless enough. Man sees a brand from a country he knows, he'd want to talk with the owner."

"Yes, but why did it have to be Orv Hoad?" Reese asked.

"Couldn't have been much of a visit for Orv. Perry said he asked for a beer twice and those were the only words he —"

Daley stopped speaking as Reese rose with such force that the swivel chair skidded back a few feet.

Now Reese hammered once on his desk with his fisted hand and said, "Jim, we missed it! It was there all the time and we missed it!"

"Missed what?" Jim asked blankly.

"Perry said Reston was mounted when Orv and Buddy came up to him. That means he was ready to ride out. After talking with Orv and Buddy he got down and killed half an hour over two beers. Why? It had to be something Buddy and Orv told him that kept him there for that half hour."

"Sure," Daley said softly. "We're idiots."

"Didn't Perry say that after he finished his second beer he rode out alone?" When Daley nodded, Reese said, "What could they have said that hung him up for half an hour? I can guess that one, Jim."

Daley was waiting.

"Buddy and Orv were going to show him something. He had a half hour to kill, and then he rode out alone. I'll bet my bottom dollar it was to meet them somewhere."

The two men looked at each other, and then Reese reached back for his chair, drew it up to the desk and sat down. "Think I'm right?" he asked.

Jim nodded. "You figure Buddy and Orv

didn't want to be seen with him?"

"Talking with him, yes. That didn't matter. But riding with him, no. That would be remembered."

"What d'you figure they told him, Reese?"

"I know Reston told 'em about his cattle being stampeded because Buddy said he did. It had to be about those cattle, Jim. That was what Reston was here for. The only thing that could have held him for half an hour was a lead from Buddy and Orv on his missing cattle. Give me another reason why he'd wait."

Jim scowled for a long moment, then finally said, "I can't." He hesitated and added, "And if I can't, then you won't like what I think it points to."

Reese sighed and said, "No, I won't. But say it."

Now Jim Daley rose, moved out behind Reese and slowly started to circle the room, looking at the floor and thinking. Reese swivelled his chair to watch him.

When he had thought it out, Jim halted and looked at Reese. "You said Reston told Buddy about his cattle being stampeded. If he told him that, then he most likely told them the reason he was in Bale — to talk to you. I think Orv got spooky then." He paused and when he spoke again, it was with a reluctance that was transparent in the expression on his square, tough face. "I think Orv and Buddy either stole Reston's cattle or knew who did. I think they killed him. If they'd got his horse too, we'd never have given Reston a second thought, would we? We didn't believe there was any rustling in Sutton County, did we?"

"No to both your questions, Jim."

"Well, here's another then. Now d'you think there's rustling in Sutton County?"

Reese only nodded.

"The Hoads?" Jim asked.

Reese nodded again and Jim said quietly, gently, "I feel sorry for you, man."

Reese, without any expression at all on his face, swivelled his chair around, tilted back in it and looked out at the horse shed and at the fleecy summer clouds in the far distance above it. Should he tell Jim about Callie and the Hoad Land & Cattle Company? And should he tell him his fears and his suspicion that this might be a front for the Hoad rustling ring? And what better person to head it than the wife of the County Sheriff? He felt a wild protest well up in him. No, this was too much to bear at this moment. Later, when he had got proof of his suspicions and had learned to live with that proof, he would tell Jim everything, but not now, not now.

Jim came over now and started to slack into

the chair by the desk. When he caught sight of Reese's strained and anguished face he straightened up instead and said, "I want to double check on that half hour wait with Perry, Reese."

Reese nodded. "Find out who else was in the Best Bet that morning, Jim. Make Perry remember."

Daley nodded, crossed the room, picked his hat off its hook and went out.

To prove a murder, you have to have a body, Reese told himself, and they would find no body unless Orv or Buddy told them where it was. That was unlikely, so they could never be held on that charge. But the rustling charge was something else. Two hundred head of cattle couldn't be hidden forever, and when they were found, they had to be accounted for. And if they were accounted for, his wife would stand trial along with whatever Hoads could be involved.

The thought of this was intolerable, and Reese rose. If he were to stay sane through this nightmare, he had to talk it out with somebody. He knew only two people he could do this with. Now he moved over to his hat, went down the corridor and climbed the stairs. Jen's door was closed, which meant she was not in the office this morning. Retracing his steps, he left by the court-house rear door, went over to the shed, mounted his horse, half-circled the courthouse and headed for the Truros.

At the Truro house Reese tied his horse in the shade of one of the big cottonwoods, moved through the gate, then took the brick walk that veered around the house and led to the back porch where Sebastian Truro spent his mornings. As he neared the porch, he heard the voices of two women chatting, one of them Jen's. He halted then, wondering if he should interrupt, but urgency pushed him on. If this was some neighbor visiting, his appearance might send her on her way. He rounded the corner of the house, and the sound of his bootheels on the brick silenced the conversation.

Sitting in his accustomed spot after his hour of morning sunshine was Sebastian Truro in shirtsleeves. Beside him in a rocking chair was an elderly woman whose small straw hat covered her white hair. Jen, in a house dress of a light tan color, had her chair pulled up beside her. The surprise on Reese's face as he swept off his hat brought a chuckle from the woman.

"Yes, it's me, Reese."

"Mrs. Crawford, how are you? Nobody told me about this," Reese said as he stepped on to the low, unrailed porch and extended his hand. Amelia Crawford was Sebastian Truro's older sister, whose husband's ranch was located almost on the State line to the north. Her visits, Reese knew, were welcomed and enjoyed by Sebastian and Jen.

Jen said, "How could we tell you, Reese? Even we didn't know."

Mrs. Crawford's hand was frail and lost in Reese's. She was a tiny woman with dark, bright eyes in a thin, chipper face, and when she cocked her head, as she did now, she always reminded Reese of a brassy little street sparrow who was watching to make sure it would not be stepped on.

"Sam had to go to Kansas City for two weeks, so I just packed up and left," Amelia Crawford said. "If I'd written a letter asking if I could come, it would have taken four days to get here, and Jen's answer would have taken another four." She chuckled again. "Eight from fourteen leave six; two days' travel each way leaves two. Heavens, that isn't time enough to muss up a bed."

"You always were a good *carpe diem*er," Sebastian said.

"What does that mean?" Amelia asked.

"Something I made up, Sis," he said fondly. "*Carpe diem* means Seize the Day, and you always were quite a day-seizer — if there's such a thing."

"I am at that, and I'm about to seize this one," Amelia said. She stood up now, looked searchingly at Reese and said, "How've you been, Reese?"

"Just the same."

Amelia patted his arm then and said quietly, "Just stay that way." Now she turned to Sebastian. "What was the name of that tobacco again?"

"You'll forget it," Sebastian said. "Just tell them at Silberman's that you want the tobacco Sebastian Truro smokes."

Seeing Reese's look of puzzlement, Jen said, "Aunt Amelia's going shopping in our big city, Reese. She wants to go alone, and I think she's up to some foolishness."

"Well, I'm not going to buy any Bibles, if that's what you mean. I won't be long, dears." She stepped past Reese and off the porch and vanished around the house.

"When did she get here?" Reese asked.

"Last night's stage," Jen said. "She woke us up, and we talked till all hours." Then she added, "Sit down, Reese. Want some coffee?"

Reese sat down in the chair Amelia Crawford had vacated. He thanked Jen but said no, he didn't. He was aware then that both Sebastian and Jen were looking at him with a mild concern. He knew that he needed a shave and that he was probably scowling.

Why, he wondered, should he burden either of them with his troubles, although technically they were the County's and Court's troubles too? It seemed cruel to mar the pleasure of Amelia Crawford's visit, and Reese searched his mind for something harmless to explain his visit. He could find nothing. His mind was too full of this.

"From the way you look, I'd say something's come up," Jen said soberly.

"Something has," Reese agreed. He looked from Jen to her father, who was watching him with friendly concern. "Counsellor, what would you say if I told you I think there's a rustling ring in the County, that the ring is made up of the Hoads and their kin, and that they've already killed two men?"

Sebastian hesitated and his lip twisted to force out the coming words. "I'd ask what grounds you have for thinking this," he said.

Jen said nothing, but a fleeting anguish came and went in her eyes.

Quietly but savagely, starting with the delivery by Con Fraley of Reston's horse, Reese told of questioning Buddy and accepting his story. He spared no details of his quarrel with Callie over the Hoad Land & Cattle Company. He was fair to her, but the bare facts of her immediate flight to Hatchet were damning. Then he explained in detail his concern over Reston's disappearance and his conviction, since they'd had no word of or from him, that he had been murdered.

Then, in wry derision, he related how Jim Daley's remark about Reston's taciturnity gave an overwhelming importance to a fact they had known but had ignored — Reston's half hour wait in the Best Bet. He explained the logic of his reasoning — that Buddy and Orville could only have talked to Reston about the missing cattle, and that it was they whom Reston went out to meet after his idle half hour.

He put it all together then in theory. Buddy and Orville had killed Reston in the belief once he was out of the way his complaint would be forgotten. It was only theory too that the Hoad Land & Cattle Company headed by Callie would be the disposing agent of the stolen cattle.

As he had talked both Sebastian and Jen had listened raptly.

Now he finished by saying bitterly, "Maybe I've got a devil in me. Maybe I'll roast in hell for even thinking Callie would do this, let alone telling you about it. But now you know what I think and why I think it."

When he looked at Jen her glance shifted away from him to her father and now Reese looked at him too. His lip lifted preparatory to speaking. "Maybe I've got a devil in me too, Reese. Maybe I'll roast in hell too for believing you, because I do," Sebastian said.

Reese said bitterly, "A sane man would resign this office, but it's too late for that now."

"If you move against them, they'll kill you, Reese," Jen said.

Reese glanced at her. "If I don't move against them, I ought to kill myself."

Both Jen and her father remained silent and Reese, purged of part of his burden, was content to be silent too. It was Jen who broke the long silence first.

"What's your move against them, Reese?"

Reese grimaced in disgust. "We have to forget Reston's murder — if it was a murder. We can't produce his body or a witness to the crime. I'll have to put that in my hip pocket until Buddy or Orv accuse each other. Proof of their rustling is what I'm after."

Sebastian raised a hand and labored into speech. "What Jim Daley is after, you mean, don't you?"

Reese frowned. "Both of us."

"No, just Jim Daley."

Half in anger Reese said, "Are you trying to protect me, Counsellor? Are you trying to make it look as if it will be Jim Daley's doing and not mine? If you are, the answer is no. This is my job, not Jim's."

"I wasn't thinking that way," Sebastian said haltingly. "If you get evidence against them, the defendants will be the officers of the Hoad Land & Cattle Company. Jen tells me that Callie has been named president in the papers of incorporation. She'll appear as defendant in court and by law a husband cannot testify against his wife, just as she cannot testify against him, so it had better be Jim Daley who gives the evidence."

Reese's sagging jaw opened his mouth a little as he looked at Sebastian, comprehending at last. "So that's the reason," he said almost inaudibly.

"Reason for what?" Jen asked.

"The reason for Callie being named president of the Hoad Land & Cattle Company. It never made sense till now."

He caught Sebastian's look of pity, and it angered him. He was the author of his own mistakes, and he would rather be an object of contempt than of pity.

"I won't do that to Jim," he said flatly. "The Hoads have tried for him already, and I broke it up. If they guessed what he was after this time they'd walk in his house and shoot him in bed."

Jen said, "How do you plan to get this proof of rustling, Reese?"

Reese looked at her almost with anger. Was

157

she trying to divert him, or was she trying to quell a bootless argument? He could see no guile in that face he loved, and his anger drained away. He said reasonably, "By my count there are twenty-three Hoads in this County — real Hoads by blood or Hoads by marriage. Like me."

"That's self-pity," Jen said swiftly.

Reese corrected her. "That's self-hate, but let me go on. Together they have seven spreads. I'm going to ride each range. On one of them I hope I'll find R-Cross cattle. It's simply a riding job, Jen." Now he looked at Sebastian. "If there's an arrest to be made, Counsellor, I'll do it, not Jim Daley."

Sebastian smiled resignedly and shook his head before he struggled into speech. "I've got a better idea, Reese. If you find evidence, why not have the prosecutor with you when you find it."

"Jen?" Reese asked in surprise.

"Why not?" Sebastian asked. "If she's there, you won't be required in court to testify to anything."

Reese looked at Jen who seemed as surprised as he was. Before either of them could speak Sebastian said, "Amelia will be here for another ten days. She can feed me and tuck me in bed, like she used to do when I was a little tad. Jen's tired and bored and I'm bored with her. Take her with you, Reese."

Reese looked at Jen now and saw her expression change from disapproval, to thought, to pleasure. "What about it, Jen? We can loaf on a horse all day and anybody will put us up at night."

"Do it, Jen. That's an order from the District Attorney."

4

Inevitably there was one of the Hoad clan employed by Sutton County, since any man elected to a county office and wishing to be re-elected could not overlook the Hoad block of votes and the simplest way to acquire and hold them was to give a Hoad a job.

Washington Plunket was a county maintenance worker. He was the son of Sarah Hoad Plunket, whose sister was Amy Bashear and whose brothers were Orville and Ty Hoad. His was the title given the man who janitored the court-house, repaired bridges when they needed it, served papers when they had to be served, ran errands for the brand inspector, cleaned the town's irrigation ditches, kept the ditch books and was the cemetery sexton. In a country where denim pants, cowman's boots and shapeless Stetsons made up the countryman's dress, and a dark suit was the uniform of a townsman, Wash Plunket clothed his big frame with bib overalls, shod his large feet with ploughman's square-toed boots and crowned his thatch of pale Hoad hair with a farmer's straw hat. At twenty-eight he seemed twice his age: a morose man, possibly made so by the memory of the graves he had dug that reminded him of the end of man. A surly, hard-drinking bachelor, he slept on a cot in the court-house basement and acted as night jailer.

Orville Hoad knew his habits well, having been in his custody for fourteen nights, so that he was sure Wash would be at Tim Macey's Saloon precisely when darkness fell and the saloon lamps were lit. As Orville rode into town that evening, he was pondering what Callie had told him less than an hour ago. Reese, Callie said, had gone off somewhere and he wouldn't tell her where. At Ty's place Callie had been jumpier than usual. She had scornfully told her father and Orville that it was just as she had predicted: Reston hadn't shown up and Reese had left, probably to hunt the rustled cattle. Orv had soothed her by telling her the cattle were sure to be out of the way by now and would be out of the county by late tomorrow.

But Callie's guess as to the reason for Reese's absence was only a guess, and Orv wanted information.

As he reined in before Macey's Saloon and dismounted, he remembered his parting with Wash Plunket. It hadn't been very friendly. Their disagreement had started when Orv had asked Wash to sneak him in a gun, and Wash had refused. Then he had asked Wash to smuggle in a file, and again Wash refused. To Orv it was unthinkable for a Hoad to refuse help to another Hoad. While Wash agreed with this, he had pointed out that if he helped Orv, he himself would take Orv's place in jail. It didn't make much sense, Wash had said, to change one Hoad for another. Besides that, his job and his freedom would be gone. To ease the harshness of his answer, he kept Orv supplied with liquor the whole two weeks of his stay in jail. But Orv had never wholly forgiven him.

Tonight Orv was warned of the crowd inside Macey's by the babble of voices that could be heard on the street. He shouldered his way through the swing doors, a gaunt, commanding man with sly, fanatic eyes that searched the room for his big nephew. Wash was, Orv saw, at the back end of the bar by himself.

Orv pushed down the too narrow aisle that separated the now filled twin card tables and the bar. The low-ceilinged, draftless room trapped and held the smoke from the cigars and pipes and it was mingled with the rank stench of the several cuspidors inside the bar foot rail.

When Orv halted by Wash, his nephew greeted him with a barely civil nod. His beak nose in the sallow face was less flamboyant and pronounced than Orv's, but he was un-mistakably a Hoad.

"Reckon I owe you some drinks, Wash — a lot of them," Orv said pleasantly.

"Some, likely."

"Well, let's catch up," Orv said and he rapped a coin on the counter to attract the bartender's attention. When a bottle of whisky was brought, Wash's glass re-filled and Orv's filled, Orv knocked off his drink and poured another. Wash watched him gloomily, content to let his drink rest for the moment.

Orv said then, "What's the talk over at my old boarding-house, Wash?"

"Ain't any. Daley's still creaking around with a sprung back and that's about it."

"Good time to pick a fight with him."

"You aim to?"

"I could work up to it," Orv said judiciously. Then he added, "But not with Reese in town."

"He ain't, if that's all that's holding you up."

"Where is he? I stopped by Callie's and he wasn't there."

"Gone."

"Where to?"

Now Wash took his drink, let it settle, then said, "Ain't heard."

"The hell you ain't," Orv scoffed amiably.

"You know when anybody in that court-house scratches hisself."

Wash shrugged. "Ask Daley. He's out on the street."

Orv looked at him carefully, surprised at his insolence. "Something eating you?"

Wash nodded. "A little."

"What is it?"

"Take another drink and let's go outside and talk about it."

This puny saloon whisky really wasn't worth drinking, Orv thought, but he poured out two shots. He was wondering idly what was troubling Wash. They drank and then Orv paid and led the way through the saloon and outside. There were a few people on the street but not many. Orv moved away from the saloon doors and the racket inside, then halted. Wash pulled up beside him.

"All right, what is it?"

"Well, it's you and Buddy," Wash said. "You told Ab and Marv not to tell me about this here stampede."

"And they told you," Orv observed.

"Hell, I'm their brother, ain't I? I got the same Hoad blood as them?" He paused. "You trying to keep me out?"

"Nothin' like that," Orv said with a shake of his head. "You're at the court-house. You see Reese and Daley every day. If you don't know nothing, you can't give away nothing."

"Think I'd tell?" Wash asked angrily.

"Not on purpose, but other things will give a man away besides his mouth."

"Like what?" Wash challenged.

"Well, if you ain't too young to understand this, here's some. From now on you'll start dodging Reese and Daley on account of they might ask you something about us. They'll notice that too. You'll start looking them in the eye longer than you have to, just to prove you got nothing on your mind and they'll see that too. If Ab and Marv had kept their mouths shut, you'd've gone on acting natural like." He paused. "Make sense?"

Wash pondered a moment and Orv could see by the faint light cast through the saloon window that he was impressed. Finally he nodded and said, "For a fact."

"Now where's Reese?" Orv asked.

"Day before yesterday Reese come up to the court-house about daylight. I seen him through the basement window. He was leading a second horse that was saddled. While he was getting something from his office I got some clothes on. After he come out and headed for the street, I grabbed me a shovel and went outside. I got around the corner of the building in time to see him turning."

"What was the shovel for?" Orville interrupted.

"I'm coming to that. I handle the town ditches, Uncle Orv. Anybody sees me with a shovel, they figure I'm changing water or some ditch trouble's come up."

"Then what did you do?"

"I followed him. When I got to the corner I seen his two horses tied in front of Truro's, so I sat down against a tree and waited. Pretty soon him and that Truro woman come out, along with a little old lady. Reese and this woman mounted, and the old lady waved goodbye. Then they rode east and turned north on Grant Street."

Orv grunted in disgust. "And if Ab and Marv hadn't told you about us, you'd have went up and asked Reese where they were going, wouldn't you?" When Wash didn't answer, Orv persisted. "Wouldn't you? Natural thing to do. But knowing what you did, you were afraid to."

Wash said angrily, "Goddamn it, Uncle Orv, you ain't my Pa!"

Orville said, "No, but I'll do what he'd do," and without further talk he drove his fist into Wash's shelving jaw. Wash staggered back off balance and fell. His straw hat sailed onto the boardwalk. Cursing now, Wash came to his feet and made his charge. The impact of his collision with his uncle knocked off Orv's hat. They wrestled a moment, then Orv pushed away, anchored himself, then moved ahead at Wash, arms windmilling. The racket of their boots on the plankwalk brought out the first spectators from Macey's and they in turn passed the word inside. Jim Daley, who had been cruising the opposite side of the street, now crossed the road. Tim Macey came out and put himself between the fight and his threatened windows.

The fight was a savage one and both men seemed to be enjoying it. For Orv it was an assertion that he was still the old bull who could dominate the herd. For Wash it was a challenge, an assertion of his independence.

Orv fought the only way he knew how: a free-swinging, free-kicking style acquired in a hundred brawls in backwoods moonshine camps, in cross-roads bars and at school house dances. He made no attempt to parry or dodge Wash's pitcher-size fists. It was part of Orv's pride that he could and should take any punishment for the chance to give it in return. Wash's blows, even when solidly planted, seemed to glance off Orv's lean and sinewy frame and to Jim Daley, who by now was leaning on the tie-rail with folded arms, he was a marvel.

The two men were ringed now by spectators, one of whom, seeing Jim Daley, asked, "Ain't you going to stop this, Jim?"

"Stop two Hoads fighting?" Jim asked incredulously. "I hope they hack each other to pieces."

Wash's face was bloodied now by a cut. He hunched his shoulder to rub off the blood on his shirt and then charged again. Orv kicked out at him and if Wash hadn't turned his thigh, the kick would have caught him square in the groin. His grunt signalled pain which in turn told Orv that Wash would find it hard to move very fast for a minute or so. He moved in slowly now, taking Wash's blows and slugging back savagely. To Jim Daley, he seemed utterly implacable, proud that the young man couldn't stop him and joyfully confident that he could cut the younger man down.

He did. His sledging fists drove past Wash's protecting arms time and again and their impact on Wash's body could be felt by the spectators through the quivering boardwalk. The watchers now sensed the kill coming and yelled encouragement to Orv. If he heard them, he didn't show it, only kept moving ahead with a senseless, blind stubbornness. Wash backed up a step and then another, his arms almost hugging his body. Orv shifted then from Wash's body to his face. The first blow he delivered after his change of tactics caught Wash on the jaw bone with a crunching thud that could be heard over the crowd's yelling.

Wash went down then, caroming off a spectator, and now Orv moved in swiftly and kicked him in the chest. It was a token kick, not meant to damage but to humiliate.

Jim Daley called out sharply, "No stomping, Orv! Hear now!" Daley swung under the tie-rail and moved up to Orv, who slowly turned to look at him.

"Why, he's my nephew," Orv panted. "I wouldn't stomp him." Orv's cheek was marked and his left ear was bleeding, but he only stood there smiling down at Wash, breathing deeply, gaining back his breath. Wash pushed himself to a sitting position now and said, "All right, Uncle Orv. Let's get us a drink."

A couple of men helped him to his feet, and now Orv accepted his hat from one of the men watching, then lifted his arm and pointed to the watering trough up street. "Let's clean up first, Wash."

Jim Daley asked soberly, "What was that all about, Orv?"

"Why, nothing at all," Orv said quietly. "It was just for fun, Jim."

Daley watched as Orv took Wash's arm and they headed hrough the dispersing crowd toward the water trough in front of the black-smith's shop up street. It was just possible, he thought, that Orv was telling the truth. The Hoads were like that. They fought each other often, Reese had told him, and said his guess was that it was a kind of practice, a sort of training for the serious fights with outsiders.

Jim half-turned, about to resume his cruising, when caution touched him. It was a strange fact but true that one fight could precipitate another. Orv and Wash had their difference settled, but among the men watching the fight there were some who were enemies of others watching. Excited and goaded by the memory of the fight, they might elect this night to settle their own differences. A man was not much different from a dog, Jim reflected; often he had watched two dogs start a fight, attracting others. They, in turn roused by the fight, would attack each other for no reason whatsoever.

Accordingly, Jim moved into Macey's and moved up against the bar. He ordered a beer and then, because Macey could not afford a back bar mirror to reflect the room, he turned to survey the place, putting his elbows on the bar top. The talk he could hear was about the fight and what a tough old man Orville Hoad was. Other fights were recollected and discussed.

When Jim heard the bartender set down his glass, he turned and picked up the beer. As he drank he was aware that someone had come up beside him, but he paid the man no attention until a voice said, "You don't like us Hoads much, do you, Jim?"

Jim turned his head and saw young Willy Bashear standing beside him. Willy was a little drunk, Jim saw, and he hoped, remembering his sprung back, that this opening wouldn't herald the second fight of the evening.

"What makes you say that?" he asked.

Willy Bashear looked like a Hoad too with the hawk nose, the pale hair, the squirrel teeth and the mean blue eyes which seemed to be carried in the Hoad blood like an ineradicable stain. Willy was twenty-three, tall, dirtier than necessary and, like the rest of the Hoads, overfond of whisky.

"I heard what you said to that fella that asked you if you wasn't going to stop the fight."

"If you heard it, why should I say it again?" Jim said.

"Why d'you say it?"

Jim carefully registered Willy's tone of voice. There was less of truculence in it than of curiosity. He said reasonably, "Well, we just got through trying one of you Hoads for murder. The night he was freed, three of you Hoad boys took me on when I tried to arrest one of you." At Willy's nod he continued, "If you can do it, name me one family that has had more kin in the Sutton County jail than the Hoads. Tonight I come close to having grounds for throwing two more in. That answer your question?"

"Hell, Uncle Orv was just having fun. He told you."

"I believe him," Jim said and then added, "So help me. I doubt you could kill him with a broad-axe."

Willy laughed and Jim knew immediately that Willy was not hunting trouble. Then he remembered something and he motioned to Tim Macey who was helping the night bartender behind the bar and who was watching him and Willy. As Macey moved toward them, Jim said, "Would you hold still for a drink, Willy?"

"Real still," Willy answered pleasantly.

When Macey stopped before them Jim said, "I reckon we'll shift to the hard stuff, Tim." Macey turned toward a bottle of whisky and two glasses from the back bar and set them before Jim who kept a glass and pushed the bottle and other glass in front of Willy. As Willy poured his drink, Jim said, "I'm glad

I never met up with your Uncle Orv when I was younger. He just naturally gravels me, and I might have lost a few teeth."

Willy smiled faintly. "You still could."

"No, you're wrong," Jim said quietly. "When me and Orv argue it won't be with words or fists."

"He's pretty handy with a gun, too."

"I believe you," Jim said for the second time. Then, as if finished with discussing Orv Hoad, he asked, "You boys still trading?"

"Some." Willy eyed him cautiously.

Suddenly Jim laughed, as if to himself. "You know, Willy, you ought to get your Uncle Orv to travel with you. He could plain scare a man into a trade."

Willy laughed too, now. "My God, that's an idea."

Jim looked at him. "You mean you never thought of it? You mean he's never traveled with you?"

"Never has. I guess we figured he had enough on his hands. We asked Uncle Ty, but he's had his bellyful of travel. Never thought of asking Uncle Orv, but we will."

Jim thought, *Well, that shoots down Buddy's story to Reese.* Orv had never traveled with the Bashears, had probably never seen the Big Island country, so his quizzing of Reston about the folks down there was a lie. Undoubtedly Orv's reason for talking with Reston was to find out how much Reston knew about who had stampeded his herd. Finding out and deeming it dangerous, he had surely killed Reston. Again he felt a pity for Reese, and he wondered bleakly how Reese could ever be rid of this maniac family he had married into.

Now he pulled out some coins from his pocket, put them on the bar and said, "Have another, Willy. I got to move on."

Willy thanked him politely. Jim turned and shouldered through the crowd and out on the boardwalk. For some reason the whisky sat cold in his stomach, and the night seemed darker than it had an hour ago.

5

On their first day Reese and Jen crossed the Plunkets' Circle P range and the Bashears' Chain Link range, keeping to the water courses from which cattle never strayed far. That night they put up at the Prescotts' where Jen, after a pleasant evening visiting, took the spare bed while Reese slept in the bunkhouse. They had seen no R-Cross cattle, but the day had put them closer against the Wheelers, so that half an hour from Prescotts' this morning they were climbing in deep timber. By that night they had crossed the summer range of Bill Macey, Tim Macey's brother, and the summer range of Orville Hoad's ranch and again had seen no R-Cross cattle.

That night they approached Reese's new line shack on Lime Creek and, as Reese had calculated, Ames Tolliver with two of the crew had finished their slow drive of a good part of the Slash Seven cattle to summer range. As Reese and Jen crossed the park through the scattered cows with their alert and curious calves, they saw that the lamps had been lighted in the line shack against the lowering dusk. The clatter of their shod horses crossing the rocky stream bed brought Ames Tolliver to the bunkhouse doorway.

Reese was momentarily puzzled. Why was a lamp burning in the room next to the old bunkhouse? Probably Ames had busied himself carpentering inside and had forgotten the lamp.

Across the Creek Jen reined in and surveyed the new building, still yellow and unweathered against the dark seasoned logs of the old bunkhouse.

"Why, Reese, you call this a line shack? It's a small house really."

"When I quit sheriffing, this will be where we live most of the summer. A kitchen and bedroom are all we need."

Ames had started toward them and Jen, riding astride, swung out of the saddle, her divided skirt billowing before her foot touched the ground. Reese was leaning forward, his right foot already free of the stirrup when the door to the end room opened, making a dragging sound on the puncheon floor that made him look up.

Callie stepped into the doorway.

Reese slacked back in the saddle, stunned into immobility.

It was Jen who found her wits first. "Why, Callie," she called pleasantly. "Reese didn't tell me you'd be here."

Callie stepped out into the dusk, walking toward them, and now Reese swung out of the saddle, trying and failing to hide his confusion. Why in God's name was Callie here? She couldn't have known that he and Jen planned to stop here, or even that they were together.

Callie was close enough now so that Reese could see the surprise and anger on her narrow little face. She halted, smiled thinly and said, "Hello, Jen. Reese couldn't have told you because he didn't know."

The two women looked at each other, freshly appraising a situation that surprised them both. Callie's face as Reese read it held an angry wariness he had become accustomed to lately. Jen's face reflected her court-room training; it was composed and held a formal cordiality and only its faint flush, probably unnoticed by Callie, betrayed her embarrassment.

Reese said easily, "Curiosity always conquers, doesn't it?" To Jen he said, "Callie hadn't seen the line shack either."

Callie looked at him and said with a quiet defiance, "A house has to have something in it, doesn't it?"

Reese turned then to Ames who had halted beside Callie. "How did it go, Ames?"

"A two-day loaf," Ames said. Now he

177

touched the brim of his hat, greeting Jen. "How are you, Miss Truro?"

"Tired and hungry," Jen said cheerfully.

"Mrs. Branham will fix that," Ames said. "She had us throw a couple of mattresses and some kitchen gear in the chuck wagon." To Reese he said, "Take a look at how it's rigged, Reese. I'll turn your horses out."

Callie said, "Yes, you'd be surprised what three men can do in a day, Reese. Come and look."

The worst was over, Reese thought, but there were plenty of questions unanswered because as yet they were unasked. Callie turned and led Jen into the cabin while Reese followed. How was he going to explain Jen's presence to Callie? He wasn't going to explain anything, he decided abruptly. County business would cover it, and he knew that Jen would say nothing until he gave her her cue.

The room they entered was kitchen and living room. Reese saw immediately that in passing through Bale Callie had picked up a small new stove which was set up now in the rear corner. The rocking chair that sat under the cottonwood by the kitchen at Slash Seven now rested in the opposite corner. When Reese saw the deal table and its four stump seats he guessed that the chuck wagon had detoured far enough to pass the saw mill on the way here.

Jen made appropriate comments and then Callie showed them the other room. The crew had cut and peeled poles to make two bedframes, which were now nailed to each far corner. New rope laced securely to the frames held the two mattresses the chuck wagon had brought. There were even blankets and pillows on the beds. The two windows were installed and curtained.

As Callie was explaining where the dresser and the curtained closet would go, Reese looked at the two women. Callie was wearing one of his cast-off shirts and a pair of his discarded trousers, pants legs rolled up. In contrast to Jen, whose blouse and divided skirt had style of her own making, Callie looked like a small, tough little waif. Well, these were the women in his life, he thought. He possessed neither, and neither possessed him.

He waited until Callie had finished, then said, "You've fancied it up, Callie. If you do any more, we'll have to give it a name, like those Englishmen do up in Wyoming."

"No. You have to be a remittance man to do that. A milord's naughty son."

Callie looked at the two of them in puzzlement, not understanding their talk and resenting the fact that she didn't.

Reese said then, watching Jen, "What are you going to assess us, Jen?" Jen waited for more and then Reese said to Callie, "Jen's helping out the assessor, Callie."

Jen caught it then and said, "Not really, Callie. It was an excuse to get away from the court-house. There's a new store and stage stop up here that I have to look at. It just happens that old Mr. Barnes hates to ride and I love it."

Callie nodded indifferently, then said, "I'll get supper now on my new stove."

They returned to the kitchen and Reese moved outside, leaving the two women together. He hadn't exactly lied about Jen helping out old Barnes. There was a new store and saloon and stage station up on the Pass road which Barnes had never seen and the County had never taxed. When Barnes had learned that Jen was going to take a few days off and ride in the Wheelers, he had asked her to appraise the store so that it could be entered on the tax rolls.

But why did he care what Callie believed? Reese thought.

He saw Ames cross the creek on the two-log bridge and move toward him, their blanket rolls under his arms. Ames came up to him and halted, dumping the blanket rolls aside, and even in this light Reese could see the quiet twinkle in his blue eyes that was magnified by his thick glasses.

"Kind of surprised you, didn't it?" Ames asked.

Reese smiled and nodded. "You two were plotting behind my back."

Ames laughed softly. "Well, I asked her if she wanted anything took up here and it looks like she did."

Reese nodded. "Home tomorrow?"

"For sure."

"Why don't you three split up on your way home, Ames? That way you can cover more country. Stay high all morning and look for anything branded R-Cross."

"That brand still bothering you?"

"More than you know," Reese said wryly.

"We'll look," Ames said quietly.

Supper conversation was an awkward thing that Reese and Jen had to carry. Callie had no small talk and Reese realized that she and Jen literally had nothing in common except himself. Isolated at the Slash Seven and at the Hoad relatives, Callie knew nothing of town talk, and court-house talk had always bored her. Blessedly, Jen dipped into the fund of court-room and lawyer stories garnered from listening to her father, and Callie, against her will, found herself smiling at some of them; the smile, however, was only face deep for whenever she looked at Jen, it seemed to Reese that the naked hatred showed.

After supper Reese pretended business with the crew and escaped to the bunkhouse, leaving Callie and Jen to clean up the dishes. However, before Reese went out it was settled that he would sleep in the bunkhouse, leaving the bedroom for the women.

Jen was truly tired and the prospect of spending the night with Callie appalled her. She could not blame Reese for this most awkward of situations, but she was angry and therefore silent during the cleaning up.

"Finished?" Jen said to Callie. "I'm exhausted, Callie. I think it's bed for me."

"For both of us," Callie said.

Jen took with her the blanket roll that Reese had brought in and went into the dark bedroom, quickly undressed and slipped into her nightdress. When Callie came in moments later with the lantern, Jen was already between the blankets. She had her face turned to the wall, but she could not pretend that she was already asleep. She said, "Goodnight, Callie."

"Not yet."

Something in Callie's tone of voice made Jen turn over to face her. Callie had placed the lantern on the floor and was now sitting on the edge of the other bed.

"I think it's time we talked," Callie said coldly.

"About what?"

"About what!" Callie flared. "My husband rides in here with another woman that he planned to sleep with tonight like he slept with her last night — and you ask about what!"

Jen said calmly, "I slept in the Prescotts' bedroom last night while Reese slept in the bunkhouse. I suppose I was going to sleep in this room tonight while Reese slept in the bunkhouse again."

"That's probably true," Callie said, and her voice was snide. "You very likely sleep together so often that this isn't any occasion. You claim I'm wrong?"

"I won't bother to," Jen said wearily.

"You're in love with him. Do you deny that?"

"No. I guess it shows."

"You want all the pleasures of a man without any of his trouble."

Jen sat up now and put her back against the wall, folding her arms across her breast. Her voice held an amusement as she said, "You're feeling abused, aren't you, Callie? I wish I could be abused by being married to Reese."

"Then keep on wishing," Callie said softly, viciously. "It won't do you any good."

183

"Oh, I've accepted that."

"Not really you haven't," Callie countered, triumph in her voice. "You can have him at a dance out in the dark or some hayloft or some empty line camp, but that isn't the same thing as having him with a wedding ring on your finger, is it?"

"You've got a wedding ring on your finger, but you haven't had him much, have you?" Jen said cruelly.

Callie's sallow face flushed with anger. "You're guessing, and you're guessing wrong!"

Jen went on relentlessly, "Then where are your children?"

"I can't have any!" Callie shouted.

"Not if your husband won't take you to bed."

"You sneaking bitch!" The fury in her voice almost choked Callie.

"I'm as much of a bitch as most women, Callie, but I'm not the greedy, heartless one you are, nor the cunning one."

"So you aren't cunning?" Callie countered angrily. "Enough to steal a woman's husband, so that's not cunning?"

"I wouldn't steal him to get his good name or to share his prosperity or to have him provide for me. That takes a special kind of low cunning."

"That's a lie! I love him."

"Is that what you tell yourself? Or do you tell yourself that you let him love you so you could get his name and his money?"

"I didn't!" Callie said furiously.

"If you care nothing about his money, why don't you divorce him?"

"So you can have it?"

"I imagine Reese would leave you half of it."

Callie's anger pushed her to her feet. "Let him try!" she shouted. "I'm Mrs. Reese Branham and I will be until the day I die!"

"Then why are we talking?" Jen asked quietly. When Callie didn't answer immediately, she said, "I'm tired, Callie. Mostly tired of you. What is it you wanted to say to me anyway?"

"That I won't divorce Reese and that he can't divorce me!"

"I already knew that. Now I know it again," Jen said. "Goodnight, Callie." She slipped down between the blankets and turned her back to the lantern and Callie.

When Reese came in for breakfast, it took just about two minutes to guess that something had happened last night between the two women. At the table they both talked with him but not with each other.

185

Halfway through breakfast Callie asked him casually, "Where are you two going from here on your honeymoon, Reese?"

Reese studied her spiteful little face for a long moment, then his glance shifted to Jen. Slowly he rose, went over to the door, lifted his hat from its nail and went out.

The crew was already down out at the corral, harnessing the mule to the chuck wagon and catching their own mounts. He headed for the bridge now, and he was more curious than angry. Something between Jen and Callie last night had come to a head, else Callie would never have uttered this jibe. In their past quarrels Callie had never gone so far as to accuse him and Jen of being lovers, but now she had done it openly to both of them. If she dared to do it to their faces, she would make the same accusation behind their backs to anyone, he reasoned.

He caught his and Jen's horses and saddled them, while Walt and Sam rode out. Afterwards, he yarned with Ames by the chuck wagon until Jen, alone, crossed the bridge and joined them. Once mounted, Reese set out south and Jen said, "I thought we were keeping north today, Reese."

"We are. When we're out of sight of Callie, we'll circle back."

"Of course."

"What happened between you two last night?"

Jen looked sidelong at him now and grimaced. "A woman's shrieking, name-calling fight. I'm not very proud of myself this morning, Reese."

"Want to talk about it?"

"Why not? It was over you." She hesitated. "She started out by accusing us of being lovers. Then I said some cruel things in return."

"Like what? You're not cruel."

"I was last night. I said she couldn't get you as her lover even if she wore your wedding ring."

"You'd only know that from me," Reese said.

"That's what was so cruel, and I pushed it. I asked her why if this was so she didn't divorce you. I told her I thought you'd give her half your belongings to be free."

"I've told her that."

"She ended by saying she'd be Mrs. Reese Branham until the day she died."

Reese said grimly, "She's a Hoad, Jen."

"But the Hoads are greedy. If they're doing what you think they're doing, it's for money, isn't it? Half of what you own would be a fortune to any of them and to Callie too."

"There's more to it than that, Jen. I've hurt Callie's pride by not being a husband to her. Still I guess my name gives a little tone to her sorry one. I've my grandfather and father to thank for that."

"Have you ever thought she could get a child by another man and its last name would be Branham?"

"That's one thing she'll never do, Jen, and for a very good reason. I'd know it wasn't mine. That would be the grounds for the divorce she won't give me now."

"Of course, you're right. I wasn't thinking."

They fell silent now. They were approaching the edge of the park and once in its timber, they would circle the line shack. It was a clear, sweet-smelling, sunny morning, but Reese felt no lift of his spirit and no appreciation for this fine day. There was more misery in store for Jen and he must tell her.

"Jen, you'd better set yourself for some mighty ugly talk from Callie. She's out in the open about us now."

Jen glanced at him and, oddly, she smiled. "How little you know about women. She won't open her mouth."

Reese scowled. "She already has, this morning."

"To us, only to us," Jen said. "She'll never say it to anyone else."

"To hurt us, wouldn't she?"

Jen shook her head emphatically. "No woman would admit publicly that another woman has got her husband. That's admitting her own failure."

Reese smiled faintly. "Now it's my turn not to think."

They entered the timber and Reese reined in, Jen doing the same. "Where do we go today, Reese?"

"The Bashears usually have fifty to sixty head of trading horses. I didn't see them below, so I'm guessing they've made a deal with Ty for his Copper Canyon grass. We'll go there, then keep north. That's rough country, but it could hide a herd. We should be at the new stage station before dark. I got it from Joe Early that they have rooms. If they're full, the woman — what's her name?"

"Armistead."

"She'll likely make room for you. Tomorrow night you'll be home, and I'll head south for the high country by myself. There are more Hoad kin down in that corner of the county."

They climbed steadily through the morning, riding single file in the timber, Reese in the lead. At mid-day they found an open park fed by a seep. Here they let their horses graze while they ate their sandwiches Jen had prepared for them earlier. By unspoken agreement they didn't talk more of their wretched predicament with Callie. Privately Reese regretted that Callie's quarrel with Jen had taken place. True, it cleared the air and drew the battle lines, but to what purpose? It had humiliated Jen unnecessarily and gained Callie nothing; again nothing was changed.

Jen had stretched out on the grass in the shade and was napping and Reese, watching her, wondered what was ahead for them. A question from either of them would make them lovers, but that was no solution. It would place Jen in a cruel and impossible situation, denying her the true womanhood that was her right. Maybe the solution was for him to pull his stakes and leave the country. That, he knew, was the coward's way, the selfish way, and would solve nothing. Besides, he would not be chased from his home, from his land and from his friends by a scheming woman who, to be fair about it, could not help herself. He had helped make her what she was, and she was as unhappy about what life had dealt her as he was about what life had dealt him. No, there was no solution.

Jen awakened and they rode on through the early afternoon and afterwards came to the entrance to Ty Hoad's Copper Canyon holdings.

This was a grim country not far below timber line. It was not properly a canyon but a high plateau between the shoulders of two peaks. It was a windy spot that was mauled by weather; the splintered and burned trunks of the sparse trees bore mute evidence of the lightning-slashed storms that rolled across it. Great boulders splitting off the high peaks had rolled deep into the flats which held meagre feed. It was, in fact, so nearly useless a summer range that in wet summers down below it was ignored.

Riding across it, aiming at the line shack which was originally a miner's cabin, Jen observed, "This is a cruel place, Reese."

"Fits the Hoads, doesn't it?" Reese answered, almost absently.

"I don't see any cattle. Doesn't Ty use this?"

"He doesn't need it with the little dribble of stuff he runs."

They rode on through this harsh piece of land, Reese picking up signs which he kept to himself. Presently they came to the weathered shack.

"Well, nothing again," Jen observed.

"You just haven't looked," Reese said easily. He lifted an arm and pointed to a rectangle in the weed growth by the shack which was not as tall as the surrounding growth. "A tent's been there lately. And why have we passed so much horse and cattle sign if there were no animals to drop it?" His pointing finger shifted across his body. "Notice that patch out there that's so trampled the dirt shows through? Notice the ashes of the branding fires?"

Jen looked at him, her eyes wide in surprise. "I do now. You mean they've been and gone?"

Reese nodded. "And not long since." Now Reese turned in his saddle, sweeping the country and the peaks above them. Then his head stopped moving and a soft "Ah" came from him.

"You've seen something," Jen said.

"Not yet. Come along."

They moved west now, aiming for a distant saddle between two of the peaks. It took them half an hour to reach the spot, and then the rocky land began to lift. In ten more minutes Reese had the answer. It was so obvious that Jen didn't have to ask the question. Cattle droppings abounded, marking the winding trail up to the saddle as distinctly as if directions had been painted on the rocks.

Reese turned his horse and neither of them spoke till they had reached the flats.

"What do we do now, Reese?"

"Why, just what we planned. Ride north to Armisteads' and put up for the night. We've got part of what we came for."

After Reese and Jen had left, Callie set about readying the cabin for closing. She stripped the beds of their blankets, rolled them into a tight bundle, then went over to the wall. A length of baling wire anchored to the middle of a ceiling beam had been pulled out of the way and fastened to a nail on the wall. She unwound the wire and let it dangle as she moved over again to the blankets, preparing to hang them away from the mice. This time she lifted the blanket roll under her arm, grasped the baling wire and awkwardly began to wrap the wire around the middle of the roll. Suddenly she felt the heavy blanket roll lifted; she gave a startled cry and whirled around to find Orville Hoad standing so close to her that she bumped him when turning.

"Oh, Uncle Orv, you near scared me to death! I didn't hear you come in."

Orv smiled, showing his yellowed teeth. "You wasn't supposed to."

"When did you get here?"

"I've been here most of the night. Now fix me some breakfast, girl."

"Then you know about Reese and that lawyer bitch?"

"Yep. Them new curtains of yours are kind of thin."

"Did you hear us fight?"

"I heard you. She never talked loud enough for me to hear her, but I got the gist. Now hurry up and feed me, Callie."

Callie moved out into the kitchen, and as she rekindled the dying fire and set about making Orv's breakfast, he slacked onto one of the stump stools and regarded her.

"Why did they come here?"

"County business, that bitch said."

"Callie, I don't rightly like that word in your mouth."

"Well, that's what she is," Callie said sharply.

"You don't really believe that county business, do you?"

Callie looked at him. "Of course not. They're looking for our beef. Is it gone?"

"It better be gone," Orv said with quiet menace.

"They rode south, anyway."

"I'm betting that was for you to see."

Callie brought a plate of meat and fried grits over to the table and set it before Orville. He removed a wad of tobacco from his mouth, set it on the table for later consumption and

194

began to wolf down the food before him. Callie poured coffee for them both and then took a stump seat across from him. She looked at him more closely now and said, "You've been in a fight."

Orv nodded and spoke around the food in his mouth. "Not a real fight, just a fun fight."

When the edge was off his hunger, Orv wiped his plate clean with a chunk of bread, then reached out for his still usable cut of tobacco and settled it uncomfortably in his mouth.

"What county business?" he asked.

Callie took a moment to backtrack and then said, "Oh. Well, that —" she remembered, "— lawyer woman is helping the assessor."

"Assess what?"

"Some new store and stage stop up on the Pass."

"They were there yesterday?"

Callie frowned, trying to remember. Finally she said, "I can't be sure, but I don't reckon, Uncle Orv. They'd have talked about it."

"Still, they rode south. The stage station's north. So's Copper Canyon."

"I just don't know," Callie said, for once helpless.

Orv shoved his plate away, folded his big hands on the table top and, rhythmically chewing his tobacco, contemplated them. If

Reese scouted Copper Canyon yesterday and found sign of the rustled herd, what would he do? Likely he would bring the Truro girl down here.

But surely this morning he would have turned that lawyer woman over to Ames Tolliver and the chuck wagon for her escort back to Bale. Then he would have returned to Copper Canyon, picked up the trail of the herd over the mountains. But he hadn't. He'd ridden out south with the woman, and in no great hurry. That meant he hadn't scouted Copper Canyon yet. Likely that would come today on his way to the new stage station. Why go south then? That was easy, Orv thought. If he didn't tell Callie that he was scouting for rustled cattle, wouldn't he keep on trying to fool her, like riding off in the direction opposite where he meant to go?

Now Orv reasoned even more closely. What would Reese do if he came across sign of the cattle? Follow them surely. But with that woman along? Not likely. If he suspicioned there'd be trouble, and he was looking for it, then he wouldn't want to be burdened with her. What would he do with her? Not turn her loose in Copper Canyon to find her way home alone.

Orv spoke abruptly now. "Did Reese know

you were going home today, Callie?"

Callie, watching him closely, said, "Yes, I told him. Shouldn't I of?"

Orv didn't answer. That meant that if she and Reese parted company, Reese would have to find shelter and food for her.

Now Orv gave a grunt of satisfaction. The new stage station was the closest place to Copper Canyon, and that woman had to see it besides. Now Orv rose, moved to the door and politely spat outside, then came back to his stool. He had to find out one more thing, just in case, and while it wasn't an easy subject to bring up, it was necessary. Callie had refilled his cup with coffee, and now Orv spooned sugar into it and stirred it with his finger. Then he asked in a quiet voice, "Callie, d'you like the idea of Reese ramming around with that woman?"

"Like a sheep ram, you mean?"

Orv laughed and said, "I could mean that, yes."

Callie said, "No, I don't like it, Uncle Orv."

"To come down to it, Reese don't pay you much mind, does he?"

Callie flushed but her glance didn't waver. "Not much," she agreed.

"Still, you're a pretty girl and young and you like young 'uns, don't you?" At Callie's nod, Orv went on, "I know a dozen boys

197

that would marry a pretty, rich widow, come to think of it."

"Widow? I'm not a widow."

"But you might be," Orv said quietly. "Sometimes a curious sheriff don't live long." He paused. "Would you hate being a widow, Callie? You wouldn't be one for long, you know."

He watched Callie thinking about this and her face reflected her thoughts. He could almost see her thinking that Reese was no husband, that he was after another woman, that he wouldn't give her children because he wouldn't bed her. In every way save one he was useless to her. The exception was that he was a good provider. Without Reese but with his provision for her, a new and different life with another man would be possible.

Callie finally said, "I wouldn't hate it much, Uncle Orv. Not if I wasn't one for long."

"You wouldn't miss him?"

Callie answered bitterly, "I miss him every day, so why should I miss him any more if he's gone?"

They heard a sound outside and Ames Tolliver appeared in the doorway. His thick glasses exaggerated the impatience in his expression. "Hello, Orv," he said. "Anything I can carry out, Miz Branham?"

Orv rose. He had his answer and now said,

"You go along, Callie. I'll clean up and wire the door shut."

Callie looked around the room and then said, "Nothing to carry, Ames." Now she looked at Orv and gave him a friendly smile. "When will I see you, Uncle Orv?"

"Hard to tell," Orv said. "Goodbye, Callie."

When they were gone, Orv threw the coffee grounds out, put the two cups and his plate, knife, fork and spoon in the full water bucket, put on his filthy hat, pulled the door to and wired it to the staple, then headed for the corral where his horse was tied. He was glad he'd talked with Callie, and for more reasons than one. The fact that she wouldn't really miss her Hoad-hating husband was a comfort and also a permission. He did not want to hurt Callie in any way and now he knew if what was possible became necessary, she could accept it.

He waited until the chuck wagon disappeared into the timber, then he rode south across the park and entered the timber where he had seen Jen and Reese enter an hour ago. It didn't take him long to pick up the tracks of their horses in the humus of pine needles tufted with sparse grass.

It was easy to follow their trail through the timber where their horses had scuffed the soft carpet of humus. Predictably Reese had hunted for an animal trail and, finding it, had followed it. When the trail crossed a clay bank, Orv dismounted and carefully studied the tracks of the horses. He noted that the horse Jen was riding had a pigeon-toed front foot; the pigeon toe threw the weight on the outside so that the shoe made a deeper impression on the outside than on the inside. Orv was a good and careful tracker and that was all he needed.

He moved off the trail then, out of sight of it, and paralleled it, sensing the grade the animals had kept to in making the trail. Every half hour or so, he dropped down and confirmed that Reese and Jen still kept to the trail. Then he would climb again to the higher timber. This tactic allowed him to spot the park and the seep where Reese and Jen nooned. Reasoning that if a woman was along with him, Reese would bring food, and that here was the place and the time of day to stop, he dismounted, moved down until he could see all the park and saw them and their horses.

He was fairly certain now that they were headed for Copper Canyon, so he returned to his horse, mounted and rode on, keeping away from any trails. In the early afternoon he looked down on the trail they would take in climbing the bench into the canyon. He put his horse back deep into the timber and returned to his lookout point. A kind of fatalism was in him now. He was familiar with Reese's tenacity and admired him for it. Hadn't Reese hunted down the witness whose testimony could have hanged him? If Reese came to Copper Canyon he would see the sign, read it correctly and follow the herd eventually. It wouldn't matter to Reese if the herd was out of his county. A word from him to the Sheriff of Moffitt County and the herd would be impounded and the Hoad boys arrested. That, of course, could not be allowed to happen.

A half hour after he had taken up his station he saw Reese and Jen break into the open below him and start the climb to the line shack and at sight of them he accepted the inevitable. Reese, of course, would read the sign, spot the exit trail and then take care of his woman. Accordingly, Orv went back to his horse and dropped down to cross the trail behind them and then, below it, still keeping off any trail, he headed for Armistead's stage station, arriving there in the late afternoon.

When the station was in sight below him, Orv reined in at a break in the timber and regarded it. Armistead had a good thing here, Orv thought. The old cabin of the relay station was his house and he used the old log barn and corrals for his horses. A new, two-storey log building lay just off the road. A store-saloon occupied most of the ground floor while a dining room filled the rest of it. By the evenly spaced windows of the second storey, Orv guessed that these were the rooms for travelers. When the winter storms of the high country held a stage snow-bound, sometimes for days, Armistead had food and shelter and whisky for them. By lying over here the stage could gain a half day either way when the weather allowed travel again.

Orv put his horse down through the timber and came on to the road at a dead run, forced into it by the steepness of the slope. At the tie-rail, which held a couple of ponies, Orv dismounted by the watering trough, ground-haltered his horse and let him start to drink his fill. He crossed the porch and went into the store-saloon. To the right of the big double doors was a counter, behind which were shelves of canned goods and staples. To the left was a rough plank bar at which a couple of riders were drinking. Armistead himself, a bald and mournful looking man who looked like a country preacher, sold Orv a quart of whisky from his stock on the back bar. Orv opened it right there, had a drink from the bottle, then said, "Need some grub."

Armistead went over to the grocery side and assembled a loaf of bread baked that morning by his wife, some jerky and two plugs of tobacco while Orv, taking a swallow of whisky occasionally, watched him. Orv asked for a gunny sack holding two measures of oats, and when he got it and after paying for it, he put his things, including the half-empty quart of whisky, into the sack atop the oats and went out. Mounting his horse he climbed back to the spot where he had first surveyed the store.

After unsaddling his horse Orv took off his hat, filled it with oats and let his horse feed out of it while he sat beside him and uncorked the whisky. It was half-gone and he drank more. His horse was picketed and dusk was nearing when Jen and Reese came up the road and halted before the store. Reese dismounted, went inside and presently came out with Armistead. They spoke to Jen who then dismounted and Reese untied her blanket roll and his own. With Armistead leading, they moved up the uncovered outside stairway to the second storey and went inside.

I wouldn't mind that, I wouldn't mind it at all, Orv thought lecherously.

Reese and Jen were the only two at breakfast the next morning and had the big room with

its long trestle table to themselves. Mrs. Armistead, a lanky and surly woman with greying
hair drawn so tightly in a knot that it raised
her eyebrows, served their food, left the coffee
pot on the table and retreated to her kitchen.

Jen felt aggrieved this morning. Last night
after supper she had asked Reese where they
would go tomorrow.

"I know where you're going," Reese had
said. "I'm not sure where I'll wind up
though."

"Where am I going?" Jen had asked, surprised.

"You're taking the stage back to Bale."

"You sound pretty damn proprietary."

"I feel that way, or I wouldn't send you
back to Bale."

Jen remembered, smiling in forgiveness.
"But where are you going?"

"I'm going to ride over to the Hendricks
Canyon. That's across the mountains from
Copper. I'll pick up the trail of that herd and
find it."

"You do everything the hard way, don't
you, Reese?" Jen had said. "The cattle are
out of Sutton County, and they're out of
the second judicial district. Neither of us
need do anything except to tell Sheriff Braden that they're in his county."

Reese had said grimly, "I want to see who's

driving them, Jen."

"And pull every Hoad in the county down on your neck?"

"They're on it now," Reese had said.

"Why can't I ride home?"

"You don't know the country, so you'd have to stick to the road. That means a two-day ride alone and too much could happen."

"Like what?" Jen had scoffed.

"Like meeting a Hoad who remembers you did your level best to hang Orv."

Last night she had accepted this but this morning she was in quiet revolt. Supposing Reese located the herd, saw who was driving it, avoided trouble and reported it to Braden who would make the necessary arrests? At the trial Reese's testimony would be discredited because the defense lawyer would claim that Reese was prejudiced against all Hoads. Moreover he could not testify against Callie. Besides that the Hoads would be tried in another judicial district; she would not be the prosecutor. Reese needed a supporting witness.

Should she bring it up now? Looking at him, she decided not. Jen thought that his dark, beard-stubbled face could be described this morning as thoughtfully angry, if that made any sense. He could not quite hide the impatience that was riding him. If she read her man aright, a re-opening of the argument now would be met with a short, polite but adamant no.

As they finished their coffee Jen asked, "How will you go about it today, Reese?"

"Cross over the Pass, then head south for Hendricks' place. It's at the head of a long canyon they'll have to travel. Once they broke out of it, they could have gone in any direction." Reese rose now. "The stage will be through around noon, Jen. Armistead will board your horse until I pick him up on my way back. Now I've got to get some grub."

Together they went into the store where Reese bought a loaf of Mrs. Armistead's bread and some jerky. He paid for their food, lodging and his supplies with an eagle and gave the change to Jen for her food and her stage fare. Afterwards she went out to the corral with him and watched him catch and saddle his horse. Before he mounted he lifted his carbine from the scabbard and checked its loads and did the same with the six-shooter. Then he stepped into the saddle and looked down at her.

"We had two nice days out of it, Jen. No, I forgot Callie. We had one."

"There'll be other times," Jen said, then added soberly, "Please be careful, Reese."

Reese smiled faintly. "I will. I know my Hoads."

She watched him ride out and then moved over to the stablehand who was mending harness out in the sunlight before the open door of the log barn. He was little more than a boy, and when he saw her approaching, he put the harness aside, uncrossed his legs and came to his feet.

"Good morning," Jen said. "You know this country well?"

"Purely perfect, ma'am. I was born ten miles the other side of the Pass."

"Do you know the Hendricks' place just over the divide from Copper Canyon?"

"Yes, ma'am, but he's dead."

"I know, but how would I get to his place from here?"

Asked to make good his brag, the boy was silent, thinking and remembering. Then he said, "You go over the Pass and a mile or so down, you'll come to a little creek. Pass it, that ain't the one. A mile or so beyond it you'll come to a bigger creek. You can't miss it because there's a bridge there. Turn south and follow it till you come to a falls, a big falls. It's the first you'll see. Then take off due south. You'll come to a shallow canyon in an hour or so and that ain't the one. A half hour's ride beyond it you'll come to a steep canyon. It's called Hendricks Canyon and you'll likely be above his place." He hesitated. "What you want to go there for?"

"I'm meeting someone there. Would you saddle my horse for me?"

"Right now," the boy said.

As Jen turned on her way back to her room she thought, *Creek with a bridge, falls, the second canyon. When I leave the falls, the sun should be over my left shoulder.*

In her room as she collected her few belongings and rolled them in the blanket roll, doubts began to assail her. What if she missed Reese? But how could she? Now that she knew what sign was left by two hundred head of cattle, she would follow it the way Reese would follow it. If she lost sign of the beef and therefore Reese, she would simply keep riding west. All towns, Moffitt included, had four roads leading into them. She was bound to intercept the north-south road and then turn north on it to Moffitt. On the money Reese had given her, she could stay the night and take the stage back to Bale. That was the worst that could happen. The best that could happen was that with her precise directions she might be at Hendricks Canyon ahead of Reese. At any rate, if she were behind him, then eventually she would find his camp when it got too dark for him to read sign.

In the store below she bought the same food Reese had. Out in the barn, where her saddled horse was tied, she unrolled her blankets, put the food in and then tied the roll behind her saddle under the careful attention of the boy.

"If I didn't have to make the noon team change, I'd go with you," he said.

"I'll make out fine," Jen answered. She gave him a half dollar for his help which he accepted gratefully, then mounted, picked up the Pass road and started the climb.

As she rode on through the morning, all her thoughts were of Reese and what the future held for both of them. If the Hoads were apprehended and tried, Callie along with them, what would happen? All the Hoads would swear along with Callie that they had bought the cattle legally and were within their rights in trading them. Reese, Jen knew, would work his heart out to get a conviction against the Hoads and that inevitably must include Callie. In cow country the stealing of cattle was worse than stealing money because the increase of the cattle was stolen too.

Jen tried to remember from her reading of law if a woman had ever been convicted of cattle theft and could not. But even if Callie got off scot-free, the shame of the charge would cling to her and thus to Reese. One way to look at it, she thought soberly, was that Reese was working mightily to doom himself in the end. Reese had said over and over that there was no solution to their situation, and it looked as if he might be right. All either of them could attempt was to do the right thing and accept whatever consequences waited for them.

The consequences they were living with now were bad enough; always hungry for each other, they behaved like proper cousins, knowing that if they once let go this was unstoppable. Neither of them could live with the consequences of that. What she probably should do was find a good man and marry him, putting herself out of Reese's way. Yet that would be cheating any man she married by giving herself without loving. She could love most certainly, but only Reese.

The stable-boy's directions were flawless. The bridge, the stream, the falls, the shallow canyon were where he said they would be, and when she came to the second canyon and reined in to look down into it, she saw a log shack downstream which must be Hendricks' old place. Looking back toward the peaks, she saw that this canyon started to form right below the saddle and that it was the only route the cattle could travel. It occurred to her that this being so there was no sense in threading her way down into the boulder-strewn canyon floor when she could travel the rim with the canyon floor always in sight. Accordingly she turned west now, knowing that eventually the canyon walls would fall away and she could descend to pick up the cattle sign. The tips of far distant thunderheads were poking up behind the peaks, and she wondered if by afternoon they would overtake her with rain.

Riding steadily west she noticed that as she progressed the canyon walls began to fall away. The boulder-strewn stream below glittered in the sunlight when the bank brush thinned out enough so she could see it. The sight of it made her thirsty, and she decided that at the next gully break in the rim rock she would descend, drink and eat. Presently she reined up at one of these gully breaks and gauged its steepness.

It was then she heard the first distant shot.

It was followed by two more in quick succession. It seemed, as best she could judge, to come from up the side of the canyon ahead of her. Each shot echoed in the canyon and then, on the heels of the last one, came an answering shot of a different tone, almost muffled. She guessed that came from the canyon floor, and now she lifted her horse into a run, forgetting her plan. At intervals the shooting continued, closer now. The sparse timber was thinning out and now, not far ahead of her, she could see the distant flats below. Then another shot came, and now Jen moved her horse to the edge of the canyon rim. In one sweeping glance she took in the fact that at this point was the canyon's mouth where the stream broke out to a sparsely forested grassy plain. And isolated in that plain was a downed horse. Then a shot rang out from below her. Jen stepped out of the saddle and moved to the very edge of the rim. There, halfway down the side of the canyon, was a rocky shelf. At its edge, belly down behind a rock, was a man with a rifle, his hat beside him. Now he turned his head and reached out for the shell belt beside the hat. With slow shock, Jen could tell by the pale Hoad hair and the blade of a nose that this was a Hoad and specifically Orville Hoad.

A swift fear slammed into Jen as she shifted her glance to the downed horse. It was grey like Reese's.

Now Orville shot again rapidly, three shots, and she heard the whomp of the bullets into the surely dead horse. After the third shot Jen saw a rifle barrel appear over the horse's body and the top of a man's head, Reese's. He shot twice and Jen saw Orville roll away behind his protecting rock.

Now Jen looked at the downed horse and saw Reese rise, turn toward the screening brush of the creek bank, take a step, then fall on his face. She watched with terror as he rolled back, clawing his way again to the protection of his dead horse. He was hurt, Jen knew, and had tried and failed to make the screening brush of the creek bank.

Now Jen ran back to her horse, swung into the saddle and lifted him into a run. The first break in the rim rock was blocked by huge boulders that barred the way. She went on and at the next break in the rim rock she surveyed the gully, thought it dangerous and didn't care. Her horse momentarily balked, then, at Jen's frantic kicking at his flanks, took the gully. Giving him free rein, Jen seized his mane for a handhold. The horse, settled on his haunches, slid down in a cascade of rolling rocks, dust pluming out behind it. Jen freed her feet from the stirrups, expecting her horse to go down, expecting to have to jump, but by some miracle the horse stayed upright, sliding and veering to avoid the big chunks of fallen rim rock that filled the gully.

When the next shot came from Orville, it was from above her and far to the right but Jen's attention was wholly on the terrain ahead of her horse. She watched, terrified and helpless, as the horse fought its way down, ever closer to the green brush of the creek bottom. Finally, in a last desperate evasive movement just before they reached the gully mouth, the horse began to run and they came out onto the flat at a dead gallop, Jen once more controlling the reins.

Immediately Jen turned right toward the canyon mouth and raced her horse across the boulder-strewn talus slope.

Would Orville shoot at her, she wondered? Let him. Her answer came when she broke out of the canyon and headed across the flats toward Reese. She heard a shot and saw a spurt of earth ahead of her horse. A second and third shot, the last closest of all, geysered earth ahead of her.

Now she heard Reese's shout, "Go back! Jen, go back!"

Instead Jen veered off toward the thicket of alders lining the creek bed that would hide her horse from Orville's rifle. She plunged through them and into the stream, dismounted, wrapped her horse's reins around an alder branch, then ran back through the alders toward Reese.

Breaking out into the open now she ran toward him. He was lying belly down against his horse, his head a little raised, looking in her direction. A warning shot kicked up dirt ahead of her but she didn't check her run until she reached Reese.

"Get down beside me!" Reese called.

Jen stood above him, open to Orville's rifle if he wished to use it on her. "You're hurt. I saw you fall."

"Will you *please* get down here beside me, Jen," Reese begged.

"He isn't going to shoot me. He's already had the chance. Where are you hurt, Reese? Roll over so I can see."

Reese rolled over against his horse and Jen saw that his whole right pant leg was sodden with blood.

Now Jen kneeled. "Give me your knife, Reese."

He fumbled it from his pocket and Jen took it and cut his trouser leg from mid-thigh to knee. Blood was oozing from the wound on his thigh and the exit hole on the inside of it was bleeding through a jagged tear of flesh. Now Jen picked up Reese's hat, rose and ran back toward the stream. Still no shots. After plucking handfuls of moss from the stream bank, washing them free of dirt, she filled Reese's hat with water and came back to him.

This time she didn't run for fear of spilling the water. She was an easy target but there were no shots. Once beside Reese she said, "Can you strip out of your shirt without exposing yourself?" Reese nodded and as he was struggling out of his shirt, Jen said, "I know you have another one in your blanket roll. I'll have to tear this up for bandages."

She took the shirt and ripped off both sleeves, then through the cut on Reese's trouser leg she washed the wound with one of the sleeves and applied the moss to the entrance and exit holes. Afterwards she wrapped both sleeves around his leg and tied them securely. During it all, even when Jen had gently washed the shredded flesh where the bullet had exited, Reese said nothing. Only when she was finished did Jen look at him. His face had drained of color but he managed a wry smile of gratitude.

"Are you ready for the news of who shot you?" Jen asked and at his nod, she said, "Orville Hoad."

"You don't know that, Jen."

"But I do. I was attracted by the shots, and I looked over the rim. I could see him plainly. Oh, I wish I'd had a gun!"

"Why were you anywhere around?"

"I'll tell you that once you're hidden. I saw you try for the stream. Is that where you want to be?"

"It's better cover."

"Then we'll go."

"No," Reese said flatly. "If he sees me try, he'll open up again."

"Not at me," Jen said firmly. "If you put your arm around my shoulder and use your rifle as a cane, I'll be between you and Orv. He won't dare shoot at you."

"No," Reese said again.

"Reese, listen to me," Jen pled. "I'm here in plain sight of him and I have been for ten minutes. He first shot to scare me off. I wouldn't scare. He has his own good reason for not killing me, so he won't shoot at you for fear of hitting me. Can't you see that?"

"Jen, he wants me dead. If he has to kill you to do it, he will."

"You've never been afraid in your life, Reese. Why are you afraid now?"

"I'm not afraid *of* anything, I'm afraid *for you*," Reese said, almost angrily.

Jen said calmly, "If you're so sure he'll shoot, then let's die together. Life's no good for either of us without the other."

"Wait till dark, Jen. I can hold him off till then."

"Listen to me, Reese. Orv doesn't know I saw him. You weren't able to identify him from here. He'll think neither of us knows who's shooting at you. All right? Rather than risk killing me to kill you, he'll pull out and wait for another day. He'll feel safe because he thinks neither of us has seen him."

"What's the matter with waiting?" Reese said gruffly.

"Because he knows exactly where to find you. Once in the creek brush, we could be anywhere — waiting for him or gone."

"Your father would be proud of that argument, Jen. All right, we'll go. Bend down now."

When she did Reese put his arms around her and kissed her on the mouth and she returned his kiss with passion.

Afterwards she said softly, "Dear Reese."

Then she rose and asked, "Can you get up alone, Reese?"

"Of course."

"I'll stand on your horse to screen you. Put on your shirt. Stay close to me. Once you're up and leaning on your rifle, I'll step down. Put your arm around my shoulder. I'll put my arm on your near shoulder, so it screens your head. We'll have to aim for the creek at an angle so that I'm always between you and him. Are you ready?"

"I am," Reese said grimly. "Only I wish I knew what I was ready for."

Jen stepped up on the dead horse's body and spread her skirts. Her back was to Orv and she watched Reese put on his shirt and hat, then come painfully to his knees and lever himself erect with the rifle. He could not stifle a groan of pain as the torn muscles of his leg adjusted to a new position.

Before Jen stood down, she said, "I'm betting he'll try to scare us again, Reese."

"Yes. Expect it."

Now Jen stepped down beside him and in the same moment raised her arm and put it on Reese's shoulder, hand extended flat against his cheek. His bare arm circled her shoulder. This was scarcely done before a rifle shot cracked out from the bench. They heard the swift passage of a bullet overhead.

The rifle, barrel down, made an adequate cane and now they started out, clinging to each other, taking an angle that would keep Jen between Orville and Reese. A second shot geysered dust at their feet and Reese spoke around gritted teeth, "A peaceful stroll, isn't it?" The third shot brushed Reese's hat and he ducked his head lower. Jen wasn't aware of it, so he said nothing.

Their pace was faster than either of them had hoped they could achieve. Now Jen looked up at the bench, hoping desperately that Orville would see her and think she was trying to identify the man behind the rifle. She saw the pale hair appear briefly from behind a rock, then the shot came, again at their feet and closer. They had covered more than half of the thirty yards they must travel for safety. Orv tried another high shot and missed. Reese, through the wrenching pain of his leg, remembered that shooting from a height the hunter tends to overshoot and he was waiting for Orv's adjusting shot. He exaggerated his limp now in an effort to keep his head constantly on the move. Orv would go for his head, Reese knew, for due to Jen's lack of height, it was the only part of him really exposed.

But Orville crossed him. The next shot whipped through Jen's billowing skirts and cut through the back of Reese's right boot top as he swung his injured leg forward. Its force pulled him off balance and he would have fallen if he hadn't had his arm around Jen's shoulder.

Then they were in the alders, plunging through the branches which tripped Reese. He fell crashing through them and pulled Jen down with him, but the alder branches whipped back into place, screening them from Orv. In a kind of controlled panic, Jen came to her feet, seized Reese by the shoulders and dragged him deeper into the thicket. She noticed that his sleeveless shirt and his arms were drenched in perspiration.

"All right, all right," Reese protested.

"Help me up, Jen."

With her help he came to his feet again and Jen saw his face was grey with pain and exhaustion.

"Go downstream a few yards, Jen, and put me down. Then clean the dirt out of my rifle barrel. Wash it in the creek if you have to, but make sure."

Orv wouldn't shoot now, Reese knew. A blind shot just might hit Jen and that was what Orv obviously didn't want.

A few yards downstream Jen eased Reese into the alder thicket and Reese lowered himself to the ground. Then, putting his hat aside he struggled snake fashion through the thicket until he could see Orv's position through the screening leaves. He watched and saw no movement, and he wearily guessed that Orv, knowing the thicket would screen himself as well as them, had seized the opportunity to disappear.

When Jen returned with the dripping wet rifle, she said, "It's clean and re-loaded." She bent down and kissed him lightly on the cheek. "I'll get our horse, Reese."

He nodded and in the interval between then and when Jen returned sleep overwhelmed him. She had brought her blanket roll and food with her, but when she saw him sleeping she put it aside, gently extricated his rifle from under his body and then took up his vigil.

During the hour he slept Jen saw no movement on the canyon bench, and while she watched she speculated on the future. First, she would have to get Reese to a doctor. With his torn leg would he be able to ride? Or should she hunt down the nearest ranch for a wagon? She knew Moffitt had a doctor but would Reese allow himself to be taken there? She doubted it. While she herself could carry the news of Orv's ambush to Jim Daley, Reese would insist on seeing him too, and while the ambush had taken place outside Sutton County, Reese would want Orv's trial held in Bale. Farmer, Orv's attorney — no, she was thinking too far ahead. The immediate problem was to get Reese in the safe hands of a doctor.

A movement she caught in the corner of her eye swivelled her head a little; she saw a moving object far out on the flats, so far that she could identify it only as a horse and mounted rider headed west. Could it be Orv? He had probably hidden his horse somewhere back from the canyon's rim rock. Reaching it after the ambush and careful not to be identified, he could have traveled the cliff north until he found a break in it, descended and headed west to warn the Hoads who were driving the stolen cattle. This was only a guess, and she made herself be patient until Reese wakened and could give his judgement of the far rider.

When Reese did awaken, Jen helped him to a sitting position, where he was supported by a thick alder branch at his back. His face was flushed now, and Jen guessed that the fever had started. She told him of the distant rider, and he listened with a curious indifference, his eyes shining with fever.

When she was finished Reese said, "He knows he didn't kill us, and he knows you'll get word to Sheriff Braden. He's probably on his way to pull off his boys and scatter the herd."

"Then shall we try to make Moffitt?" Jen asked. "Shall I get a wagon?"

"No," Reese said flatly. "We'll ride double and make camp at dark. We'll make the Moffitt road by the middle of the morning and flag down the Bale stage when it passes." He paused. "Now, why did you follow me from the stage station, Jen?"

"You're no good in court without a corroborating witness, Reese. They'll be tried in a different district under a different judge, and Callie will be tried with them. What good would it be to find them and give the information to Braden if he can't get somebody besides you to testify against Callie?"

"But how did you find me?"

Jen told him of the stable-boy's directions, of her decision to ride the rim rock instead of the more difficult canyon and of hearing the exchange of shots which attracted her. As she talked Jen saw beads of perspiration form on Reese's forehead and upper lip and she knew that his leg was torturing him.

Food was needed, she thought, and she unwrapped her blanket roll and served up her meagre fare of bread and leather-tough jerky. Reese had scarcely taken two bites when he laid his bread on the leaves and tucked his jerky in his shirt pocket. "Jen, I'm caving in," Reese said thinly. "I want to try and make that saddle while I still can."

Wordlessly, Jen handed over the rifle, then rose and moved up beside him. Together they managed to get him on to his feet, and again Reese leaned on her. This time Jen could help him by grabbing his belt to lift and steady him. When they halted beside the horse Reese reached out and stroked the gelding's nose. "He'll hold still for a wrong-side mount, Jen." His speech was oddly slurred and it seemed to surprise even himself. He looked down at Jen and smiled. "You'd better make it the first time, Jen. Turn the stirrup so I can get my left foot in it, then get under me and boost me. Once I'm belly down across the saddle, swing my left leg astride over the horse. When I'm up there, don't try to put my right foot in the stirrup. Let it dangle."

Grasping the horn with his left hand Reese waited until Jen turned the stirrup toward him, holding onto his belt with her free hand. Putting his weight on his stiff-armed right arm and rifle and grasping the saddle horn, Reese swung up his left leg, and Jen guided the stirrup toward his boot. Then swiftly, as Reese pulled on the horn, she pushed from behind, and Reese fell across the saddle, belly down. As he had directed, Jen swung his left leg over the horse's back, and Reese was astride. Now, with his left leg levering, he edged himself over the cantle and into the saddle. His right leg dangled straight down, and Jen knew that the raw exit wound would be pressed against the saddle skirt. The motion of the horse would make it bleed again and it would, Jen knew grimly, be a sustained agony. She said nothing, however, and went back into the thicket for her blanket roll and Reese's hat. When the blanket roll was tied ahead of the pommel, Jen picked up Reese's rifle, moved to the stream, cleaned it as she had done before, then slipped it into the empty saddle scabbard.

"Finished," she said. "Now let me lead my

horse over to yours, Reese. We'll need your food and blankets."

Reese only nodded and now Jen gathered up the reins and, leading her horse, sought a break in the alder brush. Once through it she glanced back and saw that Reese's face was set in a grimness that almost frightened her.

At the downed horse, Jen worked Reese's blanket roll free and tied it behind the cantle. He was silent all through it, his head sunk as if in reverie. Jen had to remind him to free his boot from the stirrup so she could use it to mount. Once she was settled behind him, Reese lifted the horse into motion, heading north across the tree-stippled flats which cast late afternoon shadows.

Reese, it turned out, could not keep awake, or was it, Jen wondered, that he could not keep conscious? His head would loll and his body from the waist up would sag until Jen had to put her arms around his waist to keep him in the saddle. Finally she slipped the reins from his hand to correct the almost aimless wandering of the puzzled horse. At full dusk they came to a cluster of big pinyons that bordered a small seep, and Jen knew that here they must make camp, for Reese for the dozenth time had slid off again into unconsciousness.

Jen took Reese's hat off his head, dismounted, went to the seep, filled his hat with water, then came back and pitched the contents into Reese's face. The shock of it roused him and Jen said, "We've got to get you down, Reese. It should be on the right side again, shouldn't it?"

Reese only nodded. First Jen untied both blanket rolls and spread out the blankets on the flat under a big pinyon. Afterwards she went back to the horse and said to Reese, "Lean as far over as you can, Reese, and I'll get your leg over. Get belly down like you did before. Here's your rifle."

Reese did as he was instructed and Jen worked his leg over the cantle, then circled the horse, got behind Reese and slowly eased him down. His left leg buckled and for a moment she had the full weight of him before he caught himself. Afterwards she led him to the blankets, slacked him onto them and covered him with one. As she stood above him looking at his flushed face, the lids closed over his unseeing eyes.

That was done, but what would tomorrow bring, Jen wondered with quiet despair.

6

Around midnight Orv, who had finally circled back to the creek, was picked up by a watcher who called, "Sing out, Mister."

He recognized Buddy's voice and said, "It's me, Orv."

Buddy was mounted and therefore ready for fight or flight, and Orv approved. He approached now and reined in.

"Figured it was you, Uncle Orv, but wasn't taking a chance."

"Get me to some whisky," Orv said, then added, "How are things?"

"Fine as silk."

"Not any more," Orv said grimly. "Who's night herder?" Buddy told him Big John was and Orv said, "Get him in. Where's camp?"

Buddy told him it was down the creek, and Orv rode on. Shortly through the trees he saw June and Emmett who, probably roused by Buddy's initial call, were stoking up the fire. "Hi, boys," Orv greeted them, and they both answered, "Hi, Pa."

"Get me a drink," Orv said, even before he dismounted.

June went over to the rickety spring wagon

out of the circle of firelight and returned with a jug. Orv, out of the saddle now, accepted it gratefully, removed the cob cork and drank deeply under the pleased scrutiny of his two sons.

When he had caught his breath, Orv said, "Got anything to eat?"

Emmett promptly headed for the grub box, moving with a bearlike, pigeon-toed walk that was almost muscle bound.

By the time he had finished his second drink, Emmett had retrieved a greasy skillet half-full of fried meat and put it on the fire to warm up. He shoved the coffee pot onto the bordering coals, then went back to the grub box to get a handful of tin cups. Courteously both boys waited till their father had sampled the jug again and lifted out a piece of steak from the pan to chase his drink. By that time Big John and Buddy had ridden in and dismounted. Buddy took his uncle's horse and tied it and his own back in the timber. Big John, after greeting his father, filled a cup with coffee from the black pot. It was only after he tasted the coffee and found it tepid that he poured all the coffee back into the pot and placed it again on the new fire.

Buddy returned now, picked up the jug, took a drink and passed it to Emmett. While the three brothers were having their drinks,

Buddy said, "Sump'n gone wrong, Uncle Orv?"

Orv's three sons exchanged glances and then looked at their father. Orv had seated himself cross-legged before the fire, and now his three boys and Buddy stationed themselves across the fire from him so they could watch his face. Big John sat down but the others stood.

Orv's opening remark was, "Boys, I run out of whisky and that lost me my shootin' eye." They all smiled at that, and then Orv began his story. He started it with the seeming irrelevance of his whipping of Wash Plunket, but that led on to Wash's information that Reese and the lawyer woman had ridden out of Bale three mornings ago, presumably in search of the R-Cross cattle. He told of meeting Callie and afterwards stationing himself above Copper Canyon on the hunch that Reese and the woman were headed for it. They came, saw the sign, and Orv said he saw them bed down at Armistead's last night. Reckoning that Reese would return and pick up the sign this side of the mountain, Orv said, he stationed himself at the canyon mouth, figuring Reese would come down it. However, Reese had crossed him up. Instead of traveling the canyon, Reese had dropped down the Moffitt road till it descended from the bench and then had followed the base of the bench to the canyon mouth.

"That put him a far piece away from me because I figured him for the canyon. Still, I had to take a chance." Orv wiped his greasy hands on his pants and said, "How's that coffee, boys?"

Emmett moved to pick up the pot and Orv resumed, "Know how it is, shooting downhill? You're likely to overshoot so you're mighty careful not to. Well, I got him in the leg and killed his horse. He fell clear and then forted up behind his downed horse. We swapped shots for maybe twenty minutes but at that range, danged if I could draw down fine enough on him."

He accepted his coffee from Emmett who then gave the others their coffee, lifted his own cup and again faced his father across the fire. Country-fashion none of the boys spoke, nor would they speak until Orv had finished his rambling account of the failed bushwhack of a kinsman.

"Who do you reckon come along then? I'll tell you. It was that lawyer woman, riding hell for leather out of the canyon. I tried to scare her off but she wouldn't scare. She seen Reese, but before she come up to him, she hid her horse in the creek brush. She come out afoot then, and I tried to scare her off again, but she never paid any attention to me. She fiddled around with Reese's leg and then, by God, you won't believe what she dare next! She stood on that dead horse with her skirts out hiding Reese from me. Then she put herself between him and me and damned if she didn't help him back into the brush. I tried to get Reese without hurting her, but I couldn't do it at that range. They made the brush. I pulled out then while they was busy hiding so they never got a look at me. That was about the middle of the afternoon."

The boys looked at each other, and it was Buddy who spoke first. "Uncle Orv, what's Callie going to say about this?"

"Hell, she won't care. I made sure of that when I talked to her at their new line shack."

It was June, the youngest and rashest, who said predictably, "Pa, why don't we get going now? He's hurt and they're riding double. We could finish the job easy."

Orv looked at him almost pityingly. He reached for the jug, took a drink from it and set it down by Big John before he answered.

"Well now, June, if that was the thing to do, I could have done it myself, couldn't I?"

June said brashly, "Then why didn't you?"

Orv looked at the other boys and said, "One of you tell him."

Big John looked at June. "You dang little fool. Reese never saw Pa and that woman lawyer never either. They don't know who shot Reese. If we tracked them down and killed him, that woman lawyer sure as hell will."

A look of sheepishness came over June's thin face, and he smiled foolishly. It was Emmett, however, who asked the question that puzzled them all.

"Pa, why was that woman riding down the canyon while Reese come around under the bench?"

"I've been studying on that all night," Orv answered. "Maybe them two figured that the herd might still be in the canyon and that we wouldn't hurt her."

Now Big John spoke for the first time. "If it was me, I'd have got them both."

"But it was me, not you," Orv said quietly. "That woman gets hurt and who do they look for first? Why, Orville Hoad, the man she damn near got hung."

The boys were silent now, each in his own way reviewing Orv's moves and seeing the necessity for each one. Their father and uncle had to post himself there at the canyon mouth in order to remain hidden. If he'd waited down on the flats, chances were that Reese would have spotted him and in the shoot-out, Reese would have won.

It was Big John who finally broke the silence. "What's our move now, Pa?"

Orville finished his coffee and before answering took out his plug of tobacco, cut off a chew and spooned it to his mouth atop the knife blade. He settled the chew in his cheek, then said, "Well, if I was Reese and had me a sore leg, I'd get word to the sheriff in Moffitt that there's some rustled beef in his county. Quickest way would be to tell the stage driver. So the thing to do now is head the herd south and out of the county. Two of you can do that, Emmett and June. Big John and Buddy, you come back with me, just in case."

"You expecting trouble, Uncle Orv?"

"Can't tell yet. Reese will likely tell Jim Daley what he was looking for, if he ain't already told him. Daley will suspicion us Hoads but he can't prove anything. Buddy, you and Big John and me can beat Reese home easy. When Daley comes to see us, we ain't even been away. June and Emmett are up somewhere south in the Wheelers getting some young bear meat. They'll come back when they get it. That's our story with Callie and Minnie and Ty backing it up."

Now he shoved himself to his feet. "Let's get some sleep, boys."

★ ★ ★

234

For Jen the night had been nearly sleepless. Early in the evening a delirium came to Reese, and there was little Jen could do to help him except keep him covered and bathe his face with water from the seep. In the small hours of the morning, when the wood Jen was husbanding for the fire was almost gone, Reese's fever broke. When Jen was sure he was lucid, she stripped off his sleeveless shirt and helped him squirm into the extra shirt he had carried in his blanket roll. Kneeling beside him, she buttoned it and then settled back on her heels.

"Reese, I've got to get you to a doctor. You can't ride today, can you?"

"I don't think I could make the horse, Jen. No."

"And I won't leave you for Orville to shoot. He may be out there in the night now."

"He isn't here or I'd be dead long ago."

"What do I do, Reese?" Jen asked helplessly.

Reese closed his eyes and said, "Let me think, Jen." She watched his gaunted face which held a beard stubble that made it seem even thinner.

Presently he opened his eyes and said, "Riding is out and a 'travois' is out, so here's what you do. Take off at daylight and head north for the Moffitt road. It's about eight miles, I'd guess." He lifted his sweat-soaked shirt that he had just shed. "Tear this into strips, Jen. Use them for markers. Tie them to a tree branch where they'll show up to you coming back. Every time you put one up, take a look back at the country you've just traveled so you'll see how it should look coming back."

Jen frowned. "Do I go back to Armistead's and bring a wagon?"

"No, Jen. Joe Early will be driving the stage. Flag him down and bring him here."

"From the stage?"

"With the stage," Reese corrected her. "This country is flat enough. It's only got a few gullies, and Joe can handle them."

"But cross-country, Reese, with no road?"

"The Fortyniners didn't have a road, did they?"

Jen smiled faintly. "Of course not. I'm a little thick-headed at this hour of the morning, I guess." Then she added, "I don't know, Reese. What if you go out of your head again?"

"What if I do? I can't go anywhere, and if I thrash around, that leg will pull my senses back."

"All right." She reached behind her for a tin cup of water and gave it to Reese, saying, "Drink this and then try to sleep, Reese."

"I couldn't stay awake if you built a fire under me," Reese said. He raised to one elbow, drank the water, then lay down and closed his eyes. Jen pulled the blanket up over him and kissed him on the cheek. He smiled pleasurably without opening his eyes and was immediately asleep.

When Jen awakened at daylight, Reese was again in delirium. Cool spring water didn't rouse him and Jen had deep misgivings about leaving him. Still, she couldn't help him when he was in delirium, and by far the most important thing was to get him to a doctor's care. She ate a meagre breakfast of jerky and bread and left the remainder alongside a full cup of water by Reese's head. She waited a few minutes, then ripped Reese's shirt into narrow strips which she stuffed in both pockets of her divided skirt. Afterwards she rose, went out to where her horse was picketed and brought him back to drink out of the stream. Finished, she saddled him, mounted, took a last look at Reese, who seemed to be sleeping again, and then headed north.

The country she headed into was a gently rolling grassland with occasional clumps of oak thickets and pinyons. When she put up her first marker, she looked back and in the far distance saw the thrusting pinyon where the seep was. She was surprised that it looked entirely different from what it had looked like when they approached it yesterday from the opposite direction. She saw now why Reese had told her to keep looking back for the country behind her seemed not to be the same country she had just ridden through.

There were several gullies that seemed to Jen to be dangerously steep, and at these she rode the banks until she found the shallowest portion and marked it.

It was past mid-morning when she picked up the Moffitt road. There were marks of wagon wheels in the dust of the road, and Jen could not tell if they were new or old tracks, or if they were left by the stage or passing wagons.

She dismounted in the shade of a big roadside pinyon where she tied her horse, sat down and made herself be patient. The half hour she waited seemed like two hours before she picked up the sound of jangling harness and the loud rumble of the stage teams and the stage. Rising now she saw the stage rounding a curve, the horses at a walk against the grade of the mountain. Jen stepped out into the road and the ears of the horses came forward at sight of her. Joe Early straightened up in the box as if, not believing his eyes, the craning of his neck would make the mirage vanish.

As the stage rolled toward her, Jen raised

her hand to flag it down. Joe pulled the teams to a halt.

"Jen," Joe said. "What in hell are you doing here?"

His lean, tough face was the color of leather and sixty-plus years, every one of them hard, had faded his hair to whiteness. He had a big nose, big mouth, big ears and, because his profession called for it, a very large fund of profanity. Jen couldn't remember when he hadn't driven stage teams.

"Reese sent me for you, Joe. He's hurt, a gunshot wound, and he can't ride."

"Bushwhack?"

Jen nodded. "In the leg."

Jen was aware that a man passenger had stuck his head out of the stage's half-door and was listening.

"Where is he?" Joe asked.

"Seven or eight miles south. He said you could make it there even without a road."

"That I can," Joe said easily. "He hurt bad?"

"Bad enough that he's out of his head most of the time."

The passenger, a full-faced man wearing a Derby hat, turned to say something to someone in the stage, then returned his attention to Jen. "What's the delay, driver?" he called.

Joe ignored him. "Can you take me to him?"

"I'm sure I can."

"Then get going," Joe said.

The passenger had caught enough of the conversation to know that something was wrong. "Driver, what's the delay?" he called again.

Jen turned and walked back to her horse, and Joe called down, "Bridge out. Got to bypass it."

"That's not what I heard," the passenger said angrily.

"Take the wax out of your ears, mister."

Jen untied her horse and set out through the sparse timber, looking back at the stage. The horses, she saw, were reluctant to leave the road. This, of course, called for some cursing and for the whip. They lunged off the road and took the gentle downgrade through the sparse timber with a speed that almost overtook Jen. Once they were behind her, Joe let them settle into her pace.

The country looked familiar to Jen and when, minutes later, she picked up her first marker a vast relief flooded through her. Presently they came to the first gully where Jen reined up. It was the worst and deepest of the three. Joe reined in the teams, then climbed onto the seat and surveyed the gully.

"This one is the worst one, Joe. I couldn't find a shallow crossing."

Joe climbed down, reached in the boot and came up with a coiled lariat. Then he descended, first wrapping the reins around the brake handle. Now he moved back to the stage door and said, "Everybody out."

The man in the Derby hat, whose fat face matched his fat body, stepped down first, ahead, naturally, of the woman passenger who could only have been his wife.

"What's this?" he demanded angrily.

"Why, Friday, ain't it?" Joe answered. His attentions were on the third passenger, a youngish man dressed in clean range clothes who, Joe had noticed in Moffitt, favored a gimpy leg.

"You up to riding maybe fifty yards?" Joe asked him.

"Maybe sixty," the young man said good-naturedly.

Joe nodded and turned to Jen. "Jen, give him your horse." To the young man he said, "I'll go straight down and then pull to the right and go up the bank antigodlin'."

Jen dismounted now as Joe shut the door, uncoiled the rope, then passed the loop through the window and back out again. He passed the other end of the rope through the loop and drew the rope tight so that it circled door frame and stage frame. He handed the free end to the young man and said, "Dally

241

that and keep her tight, just in case she starts to tip."

The young man nodded his understanding and stepped into the saddle Jen had vacated. He dallied the rope around the horn, then moved Jen's horse until the rope was almost taut.

Now Joe climbed up into the box, unwound the reins, picked up his whip and looked to see if his helper was ready. When the man nodded, Joe shouted his teams into motion, his whip cracking almost louder than a pistol shot. The lead team was too frightened to balk, and the others followed out of necessity, and the stage plummeted down the slope. When the lead horses hit the gully floor, Joe turned them, angling right. The young man had the rope taut now as Joe lashed out with his whip, urging his horses into a panicked gallop. As they hit the far slope, the young man kept the rope taut, angling his horse at a steeper angle than the stage teams. As the stage began the climb, Jen's horse sensed his job and, like a sensible cow pony, threw his weight against the rope.

To Jen, watching from the bank, it seemed that the stage would surely go over as it angled up the slope, but both her horse and its rider knew their jobs. The lead team made the crest of the bank, still at a run, and then the stage hit the lip with such force that its front wheels left the ground, then crashed down again on the flats, beautifully upright.

Joe pulled the teams to a halt, then looked back to see Jen with the two passengers picking their way down the slope. By the time they reached the stage the young man had coiled up the rope, tossed it to Joe and was holding the reins for Jen.

"She'd have gone over all right if you wasn't here," Joe said.

"Well, I'd rather have been where I was than inside it, for sure."

When Jen approached, Joe looked down at her and asked, almost indifferently, "Got your bearings, Jen?"

"I think I have. Let's wait and see," Jen said.

She mounted and again led the stage across the flats and picked up the next marker. The other two gullies were shallow enough that, after looking them over, Joe didn't bother to order the passengers out. When Joe halted the teams at the last gully and stood up for his look, the fat passenger stuck his head out of the window. "Would you kindly tell me where you're taking us," he called out.

"Don't know, but we're sure to get there," Joe answered.

When the clump of pinyons hiding the seep came in sight, Jen breathed a sigh of relief. If it was possible to make it to here, they could make it back, and for the first time since she had watched Reese try and fail to make his lone way to the creek yesterday, she felt hope conquer her despair.

At the seep they found Reese again in delirium. It was Joe who decided that Reese should ride atop the stage where he could lie down. The Concord's thoroughbracers would allow him to be exactly as comfortable there as any passenger inside.

With Joe pulling from the top, and the two men lifting him from the ground, Reese was moved atop the stage onto the blankets Joe had spread out.

Joe used the lariat now to tie Reese down, anchored within the baggage rails. Jen decided to ride in the box with Joe so she could watch after Reese. Accordingly, her horse was tied to the rear boot and they got under way.

On the return trip when they came to the last and deepest gully, Joe dropped the stage a mile down the gully course until he found a shallow crossing, and twenty minutes later they were back on the Moffitt road.

When they pulled into Armistead's for the team change, Jen turned and saw that Reese was still in delirium. Should she have Reese unloaded here and put in a decent bed rather than take him to Bale? Joe could bring out Dr. Parkinson on the return stage. She looked at his bandage and saw that the wound wasn't bleeding, and then she made up her mind to take Reese on into Bale. Dr. Parkinson's two-bed hospital was the place for Reese; there he would never be out of the doctor's care.

It was some time after midnight when the stage pulled up before Dr. Parkinson's house. While Jen roused the doctor, Reese was carefully unloaded, and by the time he was brought into the house, Dr. Parkinson and his wife were up, the lamps ware lighted and the bed turned down. Jen was waiting beside it.

The first thing Jen did the next morning was to hunt up Jim Daley.

As she went in the small court-house office he greeted her by saying, "I know about it, Jen. The boys at the livery sent a man over to wake me. I talked with Joe and then I dropped by to see Reese. He was out of his head. Tell me what happened."

He waited until Jen took the chair beside the desk and then sat down, his expression both grim and angry. The flush of his square face almost matched the color of his red-checked shirt. Jen told him then of Orville

Hoad's bushwhack attempt on Reese, which she had witnessed, and of joining Reese despite Orv's attempt to frighten her off. She emphasized that Orv could not have known that she had already identified him. She made little of their retreat to the alder thicket but Jim Daley had wits enough to imagine those terror-filled few minutes. The rest of it, of course, had been told him by Joe Early.

When she had finished, Jim Daley didn't speak immediately. He pushed his chair away from the desk and began to prowl the room, both hands clasped around his belt in the back. When he finally spoke he left unsaid much that he knew Jen already understood.

"Jen, Callie's in this as much as Orv. When Sheriff Braden picks up that herd, she's headed for jail along with Orville."

"Reese knows that."

"At least I can arrest her instead of him doing it."

"But not till you hear from Braden, Jim."

Daley nodded. "Orv is different. I can pick him up today if he's back here."

"There's no hurry about that, Jim. Remember, he doesn't know you're looking for him. Let's wait till after you've talked with Reese."

"I'm going to do that this afternoon. Will you come along, Jen?"

"Of course. Let's let him sleep the morning."

Now Daley came back to his desk and sat down again. He looked at Jen fondly and said, "Anybody beside Reese ever tell you you're quite a girl?"

Strangely, Jen blushed. She smiled now and said, "My father did once but then he's prejudiced." She rose now and Jim did too.

"One o'clock at the doctor's house, Jim?"

"I'll be there, Jen."

Daley watched her go out, admiring her slim, erect carriage. Afterwards he began to pace the room again, turning over in his mind what Jen had told him. Reese was lucky to be alive, he thought, and if it weren't for Jen Truro, he wouldn't be. Orv Hoad's attack on Reese told Daley many things, one of which he didn't want to believe, couldn't quite believe but had to accept as true. Jen hadn't stated it but she knew too. It was the plain truth that Callie was willing to have Reese murdered to hide the fact that she and her family were cattle thieves. Orv would never have made his try for Reese without telling Callie what he planned. He would never have risked her anger or the possibility of her betrayal of him if they hadn't come to some sort of understanding about Reese.

Jim knew, as did everyone with eyes to see and ears to hear, that Reese and Callie's marriage wasn't working. But for a woman to remain passive while her relative planned her husband's murder was nearly incomprehensible to him. It was a throwback to a jungle he'd hoped he would never have to explore.

His thoughts were interrupted by the sound of many bootheels scuffing down the corridor floor. He hauled up now and eyed the doorway as the first of four men entered the room. The first man halted just inside the door, and the other three took positions around him. The four men, Jim saw, were working cow punchers. All of them wore leather chaps and had that seedy, unshaven and self-reliant appearance of men whose livelihood was the handling of cattle and horses. Moreover they had a certain tough wariness in their faces.

The man who had entered first was somewhat undersized and as he coolly looked around the room, Daley saw that he was a redhead.

"You the Sheriff?" the man asked.

"Deputy. What can I do for you?"

"Where's the Sheriff?"

"In bed with a gunshot wound."

"Where?"

"Never mind," Jim said quietly. "I work for him. What's it you want?"

The four men exchanged glances before the redhead said, "How long you worked for him?"

"A year and a half."

"So you were here last month?" At Jim's nod, the redhead went on, "We just come from delivering a trail herd at the railhead up north. Last month we were stampeded over on the National. When we rounded them up, we had more'n two hundred head short count. Our trail boss headed for here, figuring to catch up with us later. We ain't seen him yet."

"His name was Will Reston and you're R-Cross trail hands. Is that right?" Jim said.

A look of surprise washed over the faces of the men. "That's right. Where's Reston?"

"I figure he's dead," Daley said bluntly.

The men looked at each other and now a heavyset, older man took over. "Why you figure that?" he asked, both suspicion and belligerence in his tone of voice.

"Your stock was rustled. They're over across the Wheelers somewhere in Moffitt County. The Sheriff there will start after them tomorrow."

"About Reston," the man reminded him.

"The last time he was seen was here in town talking to two of the rustlers. We think he met them later. Anyway he hasn't been seen since."

A gaunt-faced, tall man, heretofore silent, spoke now in a drawling voice. "Now ain't that purely a hell of a way to run a sheriff's office. If you knowed they was rustlers, why didn't you pick 'em up?"

"We didn't know it then but we do now. The Sheriff was shot by one of them while he was hunting your cattle."

"You know who they are?" the redhead asked.

Daley nodded. "We know who one of them is. He's the one who talked with Reston."

"Who is he?" the gaunt man asked.

"Oh no," Jim said gently, mildly. "We'll have him in jail by tomorrow night. That good enough for you?"

The four men exchanged glances. "Just him?" the redhead asked.

"Him for sure, maybe more. It all depends on you four."

"How come us?" the gaunt man asked.

"You start hitting the saloons and telling what I've just told you, we won't get any of them. They don't know yet that we're after them. You tip my hand with your talk and they run out." He paused. "Make sense?"

The redhead considered, then nodded soberly. "Why don't we side you?"

Daley said, "Ah," in quiet disgust. "You think they don't know the brand on the cattle they stole? If they see four R-Cross riders with me, they won't even have to guess why you're here."

"I reckon that figures," the redhead said.

The man who hadn't yet spoken now said, "You keep saying 'we.' You mean that Sheriff who's flat on his back and you?"

"I do."

The redhead said admiringly, "You talk like you make pretty big tracks, so I reckon you do. Just remember, you give the word and we buy into the fight. It was our boss and our cattle."

"I don't think there'll be a fight, but thanks anyway. Just stay away from me and don't talk."

As soon as the R-Cross hands left, Jim Daley locked the door to his office, then went out the rear door, heading for his horse. These Texas hands seemed to trust him and they looked all right, but why in *hell* did they have to come today? he wondered savagely. It would be a miracle if one of the Hoads failed to pick up the brand on their horses and then the whole bunch would be alerted for trouble.

Jim led his horse out of the shed, mounted and headed for the livery stable. He had a feeling that while things were still under control, they still could very easily get out of hand. In his talk with Reston's trail hands he had wisely refused to name the Hoads, but if he didn't get results quickly, they would begin to lean on him. Then, besides watching the Hoads, he'd have to watch them too. *This is a sorry way to make a living,* he thought.

At the livery stable the stage change of teams was harnessed and waiting out front, and when the stage pulled in some fifteen minutes later, Daley got the driver aside and gave him the message for Sheriff Braden. With it went the warning that the men who held the cattle would likely be Hoads and that they would surely fight.

He kept the driver to himself until the teams were changed, then walked him to the stage, making sure that he didn't pass on word of the Hoads to anyone before he left Bale for Moffitt.

The stage gone, Daley rode down Grant Street and passing Macey's, he saw the R-Cross ponies tied at its rail. He groaned at the sight. Tim Macey couldn't help but spot the brand and warn Orv. He dismounted at the emporium and bought two pairs of socks, all the while fighting down his impatience to know Reese's condition. Would he still be out of his mind with delirium, or would the night's rest and Doc Parkinson's attention have brought him around? The move required now would need Reese's approval before it could be made.

Finished, he went back to the court-house, filled out a warrant for the arrest of Orville Hoad, put it in his pocket, went to the Bale House for his noon meal and promptly at one o'clock was standing on the brick walk that led to Doc Parkinson's rambling old house, waiting for Jen.

During the noon hour the morning's bright sunshine had vanished, and Jim guessed that the low clouds that had moved in would bring a rain with them.

When Jen appeared afoot, since her house was only around the corner from the doctor's, Daley admired her blue dress as she approached. She was hatless as always. Together they went up the walk and were shown by Mrs. Parkinson through the office and into a back bedroom, which served as the town's hospital. Mrs. Parkinson was a horse of a woman, jolly and grey-haired. As she moved through the office, she said over her shoulder, "Doc is napping, Jen, but he'll be up when you're finished with Reese."

"That means Reese is conscious then."

"Oh yes. He slept until eleven and ate like a man should."

Reese was sitting up in the bed wearing one of Dr. Parkinson's nightshirts and at sight of him Jen felt a surge of joy. He was washed, and his dark hair was combed; and when he smiled his teeth showed white against the heavy beard stubble he hadn't yet shaved off.

"Hello, Jim," Reese said to Daley. Then he looked at Jen who had come up beside him. "That must have been quite a ride you gave me, Jen. I feel as if I'd been dropped off a cliff."

"You don't remember any of it?"

"None of it. I got a pretty fair account of it that Doc got from you."

Daley brought two straight chairs up to the bed, and Jen sat down. Jim sat astride his, arms folded on its back.

While Jen told Reese of the fat man passenger whose peevishness turned at sight of Reese into warm helpfulness, Jim reached in his jacket pocket and brought out the warrant. When Jen had finished Jim flipped the warrant on the bed.

"That's for Orv, Reese. I don't think we'd better waste any time."

"There's no hurry," Reese said. "I'll be up tomorrow on a crutch, Doc says."

"Maybe that'll be too late," Jim said. He told Reese and Jen then of the four R-Cross riders who had come into the office earlier. They had promised to keep their mouths shut about their business and Jim, telling of their plans, said he didn't name the Hoads as the rustlers. Their horses, however, were in town and their brands were there for any Hoad to read. Jim finished by saying, "I could be wrong, Reese, but Orv just might spook when he hears these boys are in town."

"I think he'll stay," Reese said. "He'll figure nobody has anything on him — us and the R-Cross crew. It isn't hot enough for him yet, Jim."

"Why don't we play it safe," Jim insisted. "I can pick him up this afternoon."

"I want to be with you, Jim. Wait a day."

Jim looked at him searchingly and then said grimly, "If you weren't laid up in bed, I'd quit."

"Quit tomorrow then because I'll be up. But why?"

"I want Orv Hoad so bad I ache all over. We've got all we need to take him in, but you say no."

"You can make the arrest," Reese said. "I just want to be with you." He added dryly, "I've got a share in him too, remember."

Jim told Reese that he had sent word by the stage driver to Sheriff Braden, and they discussed Braden's chances of finding the herd and the Hoads. They talked of other things too, and it was Jen who first noticed that Reese was tiring. She rose and said, "Aunt Amelia and Dad want to see you tonight after supper. Can they come with an armful of books for you?"

Reese said with mock dubiety, "Well, it means I'll have to shave."

Jen and Daley laughed and then said good-bye. They parted out on the street with Jen heading for home and Jim for an idle cruise of the town to check on the R-Cross riders. Their ponies were not at the Bale House tie-rail, nor at Tim Macey's, nor at the Best Bet's.

At the last named Jim dismounted and went inside. The Best Bet's customers were few at this hour and when Jim bellied up to the bar, Perry Owens left a pair of customers and came up to him. Jim ordered a beer, and when Perry brought it to him, he asked with seeming indifference, "Four strangers together been in today, Perry?"

"You mean them R-Cross riders?"

Jim nodded. "How d'you know they were R-Cross?"

"Saw the brand. It's the same brand that was on the horse Reese made me look at," Perry said sourly.

"They say anything?"

"Like what?"

"Like I don't know. What did they talk about?" Jim said irritably.

"Well, I asked them if they got that horse back."

"That grey, you mean?" Jim asked sardonically.

Perry flushed. "That bay, I mean. They didn't know he was here. They asked me how come he was. I told them about Con Fraley bringing him in. They said you never told 'em about that."

"But you did," Jim said sourly.

Perry's gaunt face took on an aggrieved expression. "Why the hell not? Is it a secret?"

Jim sighed. "No, it never was. Did they ask you any questions?"

"Plenty. They said you figured the man who killed their boss was the last man that talked to him. That was Orv Hoad, I reckon."

Jim was almost afraid to ask the next question, but he made himself do it. "You told them that?"

"Yeah. Is that a secret too?"

Jim felt a fury that he didn't bother to hide. "You told them Orv Hoad was the last man seen talking to their boss. All right. What did they say?"

"They wanted to know where his place was."

"And you told them," Jim said savagely. "How long ago was this?"

"Half hour ago, maybe."

"What directions did you give them?"

Perry looked surprised. "Why, take the

road south till you come to Ballard's Store, go left there, then go right on the third road you come to."

Jim pushed away from the bar and made the door in five big strides. Outside he ran for his horse, not even noticing that it had begun to rain.

He mounted and then sat there, irresolute. To make this legal he should have a warrant and Reese had it but, more important, he had to get to Orv before the R-Cross riders did; and lastly, he had to get Orv safely behind jail bars before the R-Cross riders killed him or he killed them. To hell with the warrant. He didn't have time for it.

Now he turned his horse and headed south down Grant Street. If the R-Cross boys followed Perry's directions they would travel two sides of a triangle, while if he rode in a straight line to Orville Hoad's place, he would travel the hypotenuse.

At the edge of town he was suddenly aware of the rain, and now he reached back, untied his slicker and put it on. This would not be much of a storm, he judged. There was scarcely any wind, and the low sky was leaden from horizon to horizon. It would be one of those long summer drizzles that might hold on for days. An early snow in the high peaks might crack it, but that was unlikely.

What am I doing talking to myself about the weather, he thought. He made himself think now of Orv Hoad. Should he decoy him into town on some pretext or other and arrest him later, or should he simply say immediately upon seeing him that he was under arrest? Daley decided then that he would simply play it by ear.

Roughly an hour after he left town the big cottonwoods around Orv's place came into sight through the drifting rain. As he dismounted and opened the Texas gate, he surveyed this shabby but oddly attractive jumble of log buildings, greyly darkened by the rain that had sifted slowly through the forest of towering cottonwoods surrounding it. He led his horse over to the tree in front of the veranda and tied him to the ring which had been spiked into the trunk. Afterwards he mounted the single veranda step and moved across to a door where he knocked.

Minnie Hoad opened the door. She was, Jim saw, wearing an apron over the Mother Hubbard that covered her lanky, almost shapeless body. The black eyes in her expressionless face regarded him impassively.

"Orv home, Minnie?"

Minnie gestured toward one of the rockers on the porch. "Set down. I'll get him." She turned back into the house and now Jim moved over to one of the rockers, unbuttoning his slicker. He started to sit down, then realized that if trouble started he'd better be ready to handle a gun. He pulled off his slicker then, threw it over the back of the chair and sat down.

Presently Orv Hoad stepped through the doorway, halted and said, "Hi, Jim." Jim noted that Orv was weaponless and his pale hair was rumpled as if Minnie had wakened him from a nap.

"Hello, Orv."

"Who's sheriffing in town with Reese laid up and you out here?"

"Nobody will miss us, and you and me will be back in an hour or so."

Orv's green eyes regarded him almost sleepily. "You and me?" he asked mildly. "I wasn't aiming to go to town."

He sat down in a rocker facing Jim that was some ten feet distant.

"I've changed your mind for you," Jim said and added, "You're under arrest, Orv, for attempted murder."

"Now just who did I aim to murder?" Orv asked with a sly amusement.

"Reese."

"And when did I do this?" Orv's tone was still mild, still amused.

"Day before yesterday at the mouth of

Hendricks Canyon."

"Wherever that is," Orv said.

"You know where it is. Don't bother to lie to me, Orv. You cut down on Reese, killed his horse and tried to kill him."

"Now why would I do that?" Orv asked scornfully. "Why, he's my kin." He turned his head before Jim could answer and called, "Minnie, bring out the jug."

"Why? Because he was trailing a couple of hundred head of beef you rustled from a R-Cross trail herd."

"Pshaw. What brand's R-Cross? What trail herd? Where?"

"There's four R-Cross hands hunting you now. They'll tell you."

Daley heard footsteps inside the room and now his glance shifted to the doorway. Minnie came through it, a jug of moonshine dangling from a finger, and turned toward Orv. She placed herself between Jim and Orv as she handed Orv the jug. Momentarily shielded by Minnie's body, Orv lazily reached out and dipped his hand into her big apron pocket. From it he drew a six-gun that he had told her a moment ago to put there, and then said mildly, "You're in the way, Minnie."

When she stepped aside Jim Daley saw, and his hand drove for his gun.

Orv shot once, and Jim Daley's hand

never reached his gun. He was dead before it could.

Now Orv, still sitting, reached out his left hand for the jug which Minnie handed him. Still sitting he drank from it, then, wiping his mouth with the sleeve of his shirt, he regarded Daley. Jim's head was sunk on his chest, and his shirt front was darkening with blood.

Orv's glance shuttled to Minnie now, but she was looking out toward the gate, her Indian's face still secret, still impassive. Orv turned his head then, the noise of the gunshot washing out of his ears. Through the slow drizzle he could make out four riders approaching the gate.

"Minnie, take Daley's horse. Go get Ty and Buddy and Big John. Get Callie too. Tell Callie to send for the Bashear boys and Wash. Tell her to get the word out to come here quick."

Minnie moved quickly to Daley's chair and wrenched his slicker loose. The seated body didn't move. She stepped out into the rain, walked up to Daley's horse, untied it, mounted and rode around the house.

Now Orv rose, rammed the gun in his belt, moved to the door, reached inside it and brought out a rifle. Only then did he look out through the misting rain again to the four riders. One was dismounted at the gate and moving to open it. Orv lifted the rifle, aimed over the heads of the four men and shot.

"Who the hell are you shooting at?" a voice called angrily.

"It's my land. Get off it!" Orv called back.

The dismounted man left the gate, vaulted into the saddle and now the four riders turned and rode ahead, putting the cottonwoods between them and the house. Swiftly then Orv turned, crossed the living room, entered the kitchen, closed and barred the back door, then returned to the veranda. Now, heedless of the rain, he moved out to the tree and peered around it. From here he could see the four riders conferring. Again he raised his rifle, and again he shot over the heads of the riders. Immediately they put their horses in motion and headed out toward the flats and were presently screened by the drifting rain. Before they were out of sight, however, Orv thought he saw them split up.

He passed dead Jim Daley and didn't even look at him. Stepping inside he closed the door and barred it, then moved to one of the front windows. These must be the four R-Cross riders. Had he scared them off? he wondered.

"I'm telling you that was the Deputy on

that porch and he's dead," the redhead said. The four riders had halted out on the drenched flats. All of them wore cracked and peeling slickers.

"You ain't sure, Harv," the gaunt man said.

"The hell I ain't. You ever seen a shirt you could play checkers on like his? Besides, it figures. He said he was going to arrest Hoad. We all heard the gunshot, didn't we?"

"What d'you aim to do?" the older, bulky rider asked.

"I sure ain't going to let him go," the redhead said. "Stape, you cut back for Bale. Hunt up that Sheriff and tell him what we saw. The rest of us will watch the place." He looked at the others. "Wilsey, you circle and fort up in the barn. Pace, you take the front and side. I'll get by the bunkhouse. Now hurry it up before he has time to saddle up and ride out."

Thus the siege began with Harvey, Wilsey and Pace watching the house and Stape riding for Bale in the slow rain.

The first half hour puzzled the R-Cross riders. Nothing happened. It was the redhead, Harvey, who ran out of patience first. Hoad could not watch in four directions at once and maybe he could make the house while Hoad was looking in another direction. Casually then he started around the corner but as he was taking the second step a rifle shot cracked out and he heard the slug drive into a head-high log on the corner. In one motion Harvey wheeled and lunged for the protection of the bunkhouse. He walked its length, poked his rifle around the corner and put a shot through the window. There was no answering shot, and he knew with chagrin that he was only being taught a lesson.

A movement out on the flats drew his attention and soon he made out three slickered riders approaching the place. Was this help from Bale? No, Stape hadn't had time to get there and back. He watched as the riders approached the wagon shed joined to the big barn, dismounted, put their horses under the shelter of the wagon shed and started for the house.

Should he challenge them, give a warning shot? He knew Pace and Wilsey were asking themselves the same thing and likely waiting on him for the first move but, hell, he couldn't shoot at three strangers who came to call on Hoad. Even if he did fire a warning shot, what was to stop them from circling around through the cottonwoods, and then he'd have a rifleman on either side of him. No, all he was interested in was holding Hoad here until the Sheriff took over the situation.

The three men, two young and one old, tramped through the barn lot to the back door, tried it, knocked and were admitted. Wilsey held his fire too; Pace probably couldn't see them. The slow rain was cold and maddening and Harvey had no shelter from it. It would be drier under the cottonwoods, he reasoned, so he moved back toward them, keeping the bunkhouse between himself and the house. Once he was in the cottonwoods, he took up his new station. He could not tell for sure but he thought the light was fading. What, he wondered, would they do when darkness fell.

It was twenty minutes later when he picked up two more riders crossing the flats in the misting rain. They too came up to the wagon shed, left their horses and tramped across the muddy barn lot toward the house. One was a big man, the other very small; in fact, small enough to be a boy or a woman. Still, he doubted it was a woman. The figure wore pants and cowman's boots and a man's hat. Again he held his fire and watched them enter the house.

Then he remembered. Hadn't someone ridden out before Hoad fired his first warning shot? Maybe whoever that was had summoned help, not for them, but for Hoad. Well, they had help, all right. It was six against three right now. The only thing they could do was keep those six inside the house.

Jen was with Reese when Mrs. Parkinson showed a man into the room. He was a big man, unshaven and partially bald. The slicker and the hat he held in his hand quietly dripped water on the rug as he moved across to the foot of Reese's bed.

"Name's Stapleton, Sheriff. I'm one of Reston's R-Cross hands."

"Daley told me about you earlier. Take a chair."

"Won't be here long, Sheriff. I think you got troubles, like me, like us."

Stape told them how they had learned from the bartender in the Best Bet that Orville Hoad was the last man to talk with Reston and also where he lived. They were close to Hoad's gate when they heard a single shot fired coming from the house. At the gate one of them dismounted to open it while the other three watched the house. They saw someone mount a horse and ride around the house. Two men were sitting in chairs on the veranda, one of them got up and reached for a rifle inside the room. The other man still sat in his chair, head slumped forward. He wore a red and black checked shirt. The first man fired over their heads, and they yelled at him to quit it. He yelled back that this was his land and to get off it. He fired again. The man sitting in the chair never looked up, never moved. Stape said the man was wearing a shirt like Daley had on this morning. Daley had told them that he was going out to pick up the man who killed Reston.

As Stape finished Reese was sitting straight up in bed, his mouth open a little, a look of utter incredulity on his freshly shaven face. Now Reese looked at Jen, then back to Stape.

"You're sure he didn't move? You're sure it was Jim Daley?"

"I never said that it was Daley. I said it was a man with a shirt like he was wearing this morning. As for him moving, he surely didn't. That rifle went off twice not six feet from him. He never looked at us nor at Hoad."

Reese cursed softly with bitter anger, and then he looked at Jen. "Orv's on his way out of the country by now."

"I don't reckon," Stape said simply. "I think my three partners have got him bottled up in his house."

A look of animal pleasure came into Reese's face now. He swept the bed clothes from him and said, "Jen, get out of here so I can dress. Stapleton, ride down to the livery and hire a rig for me and bring it back here."

Jen had her mouth open to speak as Reese came out of the bed and reached for the crutch leaning against the wall by the bedpost. Then she didn't speak, only rose, went over to the closet and took down Reese's washed and mended trousers and his shirt. She returned with his clothes, boots and hat. Stapleton had already left the room.

Reese said, "Ask Mrs. Parkinson to round up Doc's pistol and rifle. And shells for both, remember."

"You're sure he's got them?"

"I'm sure. Now hurry, Jen." As Reese struggled awkwardly to dress himself, he felt a quiet, total fury boil up within him. For some reason, and it must have been a good one, Jim Daley had disobeyed his instructions and confronted Orv, who had murdered him. There was only one shot, Stapleton said. That meant Orv had surprised Jim who was not easy to surprise, especially by any Hoad. The thought of Jim Daley dead brought a genuine anguish to Reese. Jim had been a cross-grained, solitary and womanless man, but to his selected friends he was kind and even foolishly generous. As a law man he had no peer, and only his rough tongue made his election impossible to achieve. Now he was dead, probably shot in the back, at the hands of a man who shouldn't even be called a man.

Dressed, Reese hobbled out of the room, crossed Doc's office and went into the living room. Reese saw immediately the weapons lying on the big leather sofa, and he lurched across the room toward them as Jen and Mrs. Parkinson watched him.

"Doc's not going to like this, Reese," Mrs. Parkinson said.

"I don't like it either," Reese said roughly. At the sofa he reached down for the loaded shell belt holding the holstered gun and strapped it on. The pistol was new with a stiff action. The carbine, however, was old and used and by it was a leather shell bag which, by its heft, told Reese it was almost full. A near shapeless Stetson which was Doc's hunting hat and a black rubber raincoat made up the rest of the equipment.

With Jen's help Reese shrugged into the raincoat. Then she picked up her own raincoat from a chair. She said quietly, "You know I'm going with you, Reese."

"You are not," Reese said flatly.

"Then after you leave, I'll get a horse from the livery and follow you."

Reese looked at her searchingly. "I believe you would," he said slowly.

"I promise you I will. I've earned this, Reese."

Reese sighed audibly. "You've earned more, but why do you want to see this?"

"To gloat," Jen said honestly.

Reese said curtly, "All right."

"You're being a goose, Jen," Mrs. Parkinson said kindly.

"No, I'm just human is all."

There was a knock on the door. Reese said, "That's likely Stapleton, Jen. Let's go."

Outside the buggy and horse were waiting in the lowering dusk. Without assistance Reese made the buggy seat. Jen lifted his injured leg inside, climbed in the buggy herself and pulled a rain apron over them. Stapleton untied his horse from the buggy and mounted, and the three of them headed out of town in the misting rain.

It was mostly a silent drive with the rain drumming on the top. All of them were wondering what they would find at Orville Hoad's.

Breaking the long silence, Jen said, "Reese, I've got to ask you this since she won't tell me." She paused. "Did Callie come to see you this afternoon?"

"No. She probably didn't know about the shooting, Jen."

"She knew," Jen said quietly. "I sent a stable boy out to tell her this morning. He saw her and delivered the message."

"It doesn't matter."

271

"Especially to her," Jen said bitterly.

It was full dark as they approached the lightless shack of Orville Hoad's. They picked up the sound of sporadic gunfire long before they could make out the tall cotton-woods around the house.

The darkness was almost total, made so by the sifting rain, so that they rode up to the gate and still could not see the house. Stape moved away from them and called into the night, "Pace, you around?"

A gunshot from the cottonwoods broke the silence, and on the heels of it a voice called out, "Stape, over here." Then he added anxiously, "You got help?"

"The Sheriff," Stape said laconically. Now Reese pulled in behind Stape's horse and stopped when it did. Stape and Pace moved up to the buggy and halted.

"This here's Pace, Sheriff. Anybody make a break from the house, Pace?"

"Not this side. But Wilsey back in the barn's been shooting. So has Harvey."

"How many are in there?" Reese asked.

"They been shooting from four sides of the house at the same time, so at least four."

"Any talk back and forth?"

"No. Just shooting. Not so much from them lately either."

"Shoot at anyone who tries to leave, Pace."

"That's what I'm hoping for."

"Stapleton, lead me to your other partners."

Again Stape put his horse in motion, following the fence and turning when it did. They were in the cottonwoods now, and this time they were picked up by Harvey. "Stape, sing out."

"It's me and the Sheriff," Stape called. In a moment Harvey appeared by the fence, and Reese asked again if anyone had tried for a break.

"Two of them," Harvey said. "One's down out there now. The other was knocked down, but he made it back. Now I got to get back, Sheriff." They heard him move off into the night, heard the sound of his footsteps stop, then return. "They got mighty quiet in there, Sheriff. D'you think they're planning a rush for their horses?"

"Maybe they're low on ammunition."

"Maybe. But at first they were shooting like they was making it in there." Again they heard him move off.

Reese said, "Now take me to the last man."

Stape now passed the fence, circled around and pulled up behind the log barn. Stape went inside, calling, "Wilsey. It's me, Stape. Wilsey, sing out."

Then Reese and Jen heard two men talking

and afterwards Stape appeared beside the buggy. "Why don't you drive it inside, Sheriff. Wilsey don't want to leave his post. I'll open the door."

Reese waited until he heard Stape's call, and then he turned the horse toward the barn, trusting him to find the door in the blackness.

Once inside Reese wrapped the reins around the whip stock, then by feel loaded the carbine. Afterwards, in the pitch blackness, Jen helped him down. Then Stape led them toward the door in the front of the barn. Stape said over his shoulder, "Wilsey brought in all their horses through a side door after it got dark. They're off to the right so watch it."

Afterward they reached Wilsey who was standing just back of the door, whose other half was open. "Keep behind me, Sheriff," Wilsey warned. "I've been shooting from up by the loading door, but they may figure I've shifted."

"One man down?" Reese asked.

"One down and one hurt."

"How many are in there?" Reese asked.

"One loner, a big woman, made the seventh, counting Hoad."

That would be Minnie, Reese thought. She would have rounded up the boys and probably Ty and Buddy. Reese considered now. Orv would know that he was being besieged by four men, no more. Of his own seven men, one might be dead, another wounded. That would leave his five, counting Minnie, against the four. One of the four, Wilsey, stood between him and the horses the Hoads needed. Twice the Hoads had made a try for the barn and lost. Orv, as always, wouldn't accept this defeat but what did he plan? If he waited until daylight his plight would be worse, since he would think that one of the R-Cross riders would alert the town and he would face a posse after daylight. Surely then, alone or with all the others, he would rush the wagon shed and adjoining corral for the horses necessary to his escape. He would not know that as of now there were three riflemen in the barn instead of one. Accordingly it would be foolish for Reese to reveal his own presence by trying to persuade Orv to surrender. Still, wasn't that his duty?

His thoughts were interrupted by Wilsey. "Stape, you take the door here. I'll head up the loft to the loading door." He vanished and they heard him climb the wooden ladder to the hayloft. Jen said then, "What are you thinking, Reese?"

"That if I keep my mouth shut they'll think there's only one man here. They might take a chance and rush it."

"You'll kill some of them," Jen said quietly.

"So I'd better call out to Orv and tell him fifty men are on their way I'd better tell him —"

Wilsey yelled from above, "Here they come, Stape!" and he began to shoot. Harvey back of the bunkhouse joined in. Stape now kneeled down and started shooting around the door. Reese spun Jen roughly back against the log wall.

It sounded to Reese as if all the Hoads were shooting for a fusillade poured into the barn from the barn lot. From the angle at which Stape was shooting Reese guessed that all the Hoads were headed for the adjoining wagon shed, where they had left their horses that Wilsey cunningly had led through the side door from the wagon shed into the barn. From outside now came howls of rage or pain, Reese couldn't tell which. He picked up a vicious cursing that came from the wagon shed. Now Reese drew his six-gun, hobbled away from Jen and faced where he guessed the side door from the wagon shed was. It opened now with a crash, and Reese shot chest high at only the sound of footfalls charging through the door. On the heel of his shot came a great grunting, strangled cough and he heard Wilsey call, "Hold it! Hold it!"

From the barn lot came Buddy's shrill cry, "We quit! We quit, don't shoot! We quit!"

Reese heard Wilsey yell, "Throw down your guns. Come up to the barn door."

Reese reached in his pocket, drew out a match and wiped it alight on his crutch. By its light he saw Orville Hoad face down on the dirt floor some eight feet inside the barn. Reese looked about him now, saw a lantern hanging from a stall timber and hobbling over to it, he took it down, sprung the chimney and lighted its wick.

Stape had risen now and stepped out into the night. Reese's glance shifted to Jen. The fright was fading from her face, Reese saw. Now, his pistol long since holstered, he lurched toward the door, the lantern in his hand. As he stepped out into the night he held the lantern high. He could make out three forms lying in the barn lot. His glance shifted to the door where he saw Ty and Buddy leaning against it. Buddy was cradling his arm by the palm of his other hand, and his head was hung. Ty only stared down at the mud.

Wilsey now called down from the loft door, "Them three out there ain't moved, Sheriff, but don't be surprised if I have to shoot."

Reese felt Jen come up beside him, and now he turned and headed into the barn lot toward the prone slickered figures. Just within range of the lantern light he could see Harvey, rifle dangling from his hand, coming toward him. The first figure was that of Wash Plunket, lying face up and lifeless. Beyond him was Big John, his face so deeply buried in the mud that he could not be alive.

Now Reese moved to the third body, and when he approached he felt a wild and dreadful premonition. He lunged desperately to close the distance, and then he halted, holding the lantern high.

It was Callie, her sightless eyes unblinking in the slow rain.

He tried to kneel and could not, but Jen knelt for him, touching Callie's face first, then lifting her arm and feeling the wrist for the pulse. Then she looked up at Reese and shook her head in negation.

Reese stared dumbly at Callie, trying to comprehend this. The rain hissed softly on the lantern glass and Reese was aware that someone had come up beside him.

"Christ! A woman! My God, I didn't know! I was sound shootin'."

"You couldn't know," Reese said, never taking his glance from Callie's thin, child's face. It was oddly serene in death, he thought, as if she were relieved that her quarrel with him and with her own world was blessedly over.

He was aware now that Minnie had come out of the house and was approaching. When she halted before him she asked, "Where's Orv?"

"Dead." Now Reese gestured with the lantern toward Callie. "Why did you let her go?"

"Because she held a gun on me."

He was aware now that Jen was shrugging out of her raincoat, and he watched as she spread it over Callie, covering her face. It was a kind gesture, a last gesture from the woman he could now marry.

The employees of THORNDIKE PRESS hope you have enjoyed this Large Print book. All our Large Print titles are designed for easy reading, and all our books are made to last. Other Thorndike Large Print books are available at your library, through selected bookstores, or directly from us. For more information about current and upcoming titles, please call or mail your name and address to:

THORNDIKE PRESS
PO Box 159
Thorndike, Maine 04986
800/223-6121
207/948-2962

ACB
7-3-2000